Marinated Conditions

Eugeena Patterson Mystery, Book 7

Tyora Moody

Tymm Publishing LLC

Marinated Conditions

A Eugeena Patterson Mystery, Book 7

Copyright © 2024 by Tyora Moody

Published by Tymm Publishing LLC
www.tymmpublishing.com

Paperback ISBN: 978-1-961437-18-0
Ebook ISBN: 978-1-961437-17-3

Cover Design: TywebbinCreations.com
Editing: Felicia Murrell

Chapter 1

I didn't have to look at my watch to know that breakfast had been a few hours ago. When it was time to eat, my body had a way of letting me know. I suddenly started thinking so hard about food, I could almost taste it. I have always had a love affair with food and mealtimes were like sharing time with an old friend. Lately, when I found myself thinking about certain types of food, fond memories accompanied those thoughts.

There was always plenty of good cooking growing up in the Lowcountry. My earliest memories were of me sitting at the kitchen table while my mama baked or prepared dinner. She seemed to cook something special every night, and not just on Sunday. I imagine it's why I spent so much time in the kitchen as an adult. It was the closest activity I had that connected me to my mama who'd passed when I was twelve years old.

Last night, my only daughter, Leesa brought her kids over and we spent time talking about her upcoming nuptials. Leesa and I have come a long way from the bickering mother and daughter we used to be to having more understanding about each other as women. I'd missed out on having my mama around when I was Leesa's age, so I truly treasured watching my baby girl. Even though she was a mother of two, the past few months I enjoyed seeing her relive the childlike wonder of that little girl who dreamed aloud about her future wedding. Only this was no dream, it was for real. Getting married had been a long time coming for Leesa, and I was proud of this next step in her life.

From the moment her fiancé Chris Black proposed last June, Leesa dived into planning for their wedding.

MARINATED CONDITIONS

They'd both agreed on a yearlong engagement. Since the beginning of the year, we'd met every week for lunch and then gathered at least one weekend a month with Leesa's besties. Hard to believe the wedding was almost two months away.

Today was Friday, and Leesa wanted to meet with the caterer to confirm the menu. I stepped outside and sat in a rocking chair on the front porch to wait for her arrival. It was the perfect day for being outdoors. The April weather had been breezy all week. Best enjoy it, summer temperatures along with high humidity would barge in before its designated time. Spring seemed to last only a few weeks in the South despite the calendar dates.

My husband, Amos Jones, whipped around the front yard on his favorite toy. I grinned and waved at him. I'd never imagined I would marry again after my first husband passed. A widow himself, Amos used to live next door. He had become the neighborhood yard guy and grabbed my attention, reminding me that life wasn't over. Sure, I was a retired widow and an empty nester, but I learned fast that my hormones were still working just fine.

Amos eased up close to the front porch on his lawn-mower and cut the engine. "Where y'all heading to-day?"

"Smokin' Ward. You know Leesa's friends have been catering for a while, but they acquired a food truck a year ago."

Amos swung his legs around on the lawnmower and stood. "Yeah. And they serve barbecue, right?"

I nodded. Another one of my favorite memories involved my father, a quiet and reserved man, somewhat like Amos. My dad and his brothers would smoke a whole hog out in the backyard, one of the benefits of living out in the country. He cooked some of the best barbecue. To this day, I was still biased to my daddy's cooking.

I explained to Amos. "Smokin' Ward specializes in giving people the barbecue they like best, whether it's vinegar based or tomato based. Leesa said they won a culinary award. Want me to bring you a plate back?"

Amos wiped his brow with a handkerchief. "Yes, ma'am. I will be ready for some down home cooking after I finish these yards. Make sure they add some hash and rice, too."

Amos claimed he was a city boy, but that man loved to eat good ole country food. I knew he was working up quite an appetite. His daughter was now living in the house he still owned next door, and Amos kept both lawns nice and neat. He even helped out our next door neighbor, Louise Hopkins.

Speaking of Louise, I spotted her silver hair first from her porch. Louise had a brief stint in the nursing home before she returned to her home in Sugar Creek. Now, her granddaughter, Joss Miller, lived with her. Louise waved to me. "Hey, Eugeena."

"How you doing, Louise? You want some barbecue?"

Louise clapped her hands together like she was much younger than her seventy some years. "Oooh, that sounds so good."

"We'll bring you back something." I grew up in the era where you took care of your neighbors. I turned to see Leesa pull her minivan into our driveway. "Well, there's the bride. I didn't know how super organized that child was until she started handing out tasks to do for this wedding." I stood from the rocking chair and made my way down the steps. "That girl has a checklist for everything."

Amos grabbed my hand and helped me down the last few steps. "Like mother, like daughter. You love your notebooks too," he grinned.

I threw my head back and laughed. "That's true."

I walked over and opened the passenger side door. My daughter leaned forward and waved at Amos who'd followed behind me. "Hey, Amos," Leesa said. "You have these yards looking so good."

"Thank you. I appreciate the compliment." Amos said, holding the door open for me. "So I hear you are having barbecue at your wedding?"

Leesa grinned. "My friend Sasha and her husband are excellent cooks. We're going to have a whole soul food menu. Both Chris's family and mine love to eat."

"We absolutely do." I agreed as I climbed into her minivan.

Amos waved and headed back toward his lawn-mower.

I waited until Leesa backed out of the driveway. "How long do you have for lunch today? Are we going to be able to get everything accomplished?"

A big grin stretched across her face. "No worries. I have the afternoon off."

I raised an eyebrow. "Well, that sounds like a plan."

Within a few minutes, we reached the Sugar Creek business district. Across the street was Sugar Creek Café and a few shops. Leesa passed them and turned into a parking lot next to a furniture store.

Before I opened the car door, I could smell the savory aroma of smoked barbecue in the air. My stomach rumbled, already tasting the sweet and tangy sauce that would soon coat my fingers. "Mmmm, it smells good out here."

We rounded the corner of the parking lot, and I saw the BBQ Fixin' food truck. That struck me as odd. "I thought we were going to Sasha's truck."

Leesa frowned. "It's over there. You know what? Sasha told me last night that the guy who owns BBQ

Fixin' has been setting up shop wherever they are lately. She said it was weird. Sasha and her husband, Marcus, book with businesses and organizations in advance to be able to sell food. No one wants two barbecue food trucks in the same location."

"That is weird. Sounds like someone is trying to strike up a bit of competition."

Leesa said, "Well, the BBQ Fixin' food truck has won some awards in the past. Sasha said the truck had been off the scene awhile."

I looked over at the BBQ Fixin' truck. It was black with red lettering on the side. There wasn't a lot of activity, nor was the concession window open.

The Smokin' Ward truck came into view. You couldn't miss it. Red like a fire truck with bright gold and white lettering, I noticed it wasn't a typical food truck, but more like a trailer. A pretty long trailer with a porch on the back. This was the first time I'd seen it up close, although Leesa talked about her friend's business all the time.

"Wow. Their truck is huge. It's like the ones I've seen at festivals and the farmers market."

Leesa nodded. "They saved up their money and had it customized. It has everything in it, including a bathroom. Marcus likes to travel and do competitions. They've done at least three in the past year."

As we approached, we were greeted with a wave and a smile from the young woman in the concession window. "Hey, y'all!" She said, "We're opening."

Usually when I saw Sasha Greene, she wore her thick curly hair in a fierce fro. Today, it was tied back with an emerald scarf. Her hair had always been deep auburn, even when she was younger. I could tell she'd added a bit more red to her natural coloring. It was good that Leesa remained in touch with a childhood friend.

Leesa walked up to the window and pointed toward the other food truck. "Hey, Sasha. Why are they here?"

Sasha shook her head. "I don't know. His truck was here when we arrived. Marcus is going to tell Darren to move his truck. This is the second time this week that he's pulled this stunt. There is plenty of room for both of our trucks to serve food in Charleston.

He could have chosen another location. We've been setting up here every Friday for the past few months. The businesses and their customers provide great foot traffic."

I turned around and caught sight of Marcus striding over to the other food truck. "Are you sure it's a good idea for Marcus to go over there? That guy might be itching to start a fight."

Sasha's face scrunched up as she bit her lip. "I tried to stop him, but you know men." She squinted. "Well, it looks like he's coming back."

Marcus Green sprinted across the parking lot back to where we stood by the Smokin' Ward truck. His face appeared strained.

"Marcus, is everything okay?" I asked.

Leesa added, "Yeah, was that guy giving you a hard time?"

Marcus stopped and put his hands on his hips. Then he bent down like he was about to hyperventilate.

"Honey, are you okay?" A concerned Sasha moved quickly to the side door of the food trailer and climbed out. We all stood around Marcus wondering what was wrong.

Finally, sounding out of breath, he said. "I went over to ask Darren to move his truck. He didn't answer, so I walked around and the truck's back door was wide open. We may need to call 911."

"Oh," I said. "Is he hurt?" I reached into my bag and pulled out my phone. "Well, what should we tell them?"

Marcus shook his head. "I don't know. He looks like he's not breathing. And there's—"

"What?" Leesa and I yelled at the same time.

Before I could stop her, Leesa started walking toward the BBQ Fixin' truck. "Leesa," I shouted, scurrying behind her. "Where are you going?"

"To see if the man needs help. I took a CPR class a few months ago."

"Yes, I remember you telling me that."

Leesa said, "Well, if he's not breathing, it could be too late by the time the ambulance gets here."

We reached the truck and hurried around to the back. But before we reached the open doors, I saw two large feet dressed in white sneakers. Then the man's large body sprawled out on the food truck's floor came into view. I grabbed Leesa and yanked her back. I didn't know what was more convincing, the blood pooling under the man's head or the bluish tinge of his skin.

Probably both.

"Leesa, CPR isn't going to help him. We need to call 911 and stay back."

This is a crime scene.

Chapter 2

Not sure why, but the smell wasn't noticeable until we drew closer to the BBQ Fixin' truck. Leesa gagged and covered her mouth, her eyes wide with horror. Without a word, we turned and hurried back to Sasha and Marcus. I could hear my heart pounding in my chest.

Not a dead body! Why, Lord?

We huddled together, not talking. Sasha and Marcus both appeared to be in shock, while Leesa kept looking at me like I knew what to do. I dialed 911. My trembling fingers struggled to hit the right numbers to report finding a man dead in his own food truck.

I'd seen my share of dead bodies over the past few years. For whatever reason, I seemed to stumble upon crimes. Even on my honeymoon last summer with Amos, we found ourselves caught up in a crime that involved my childhood friend.

A police car screeched to a halt, its red and blue lights flashing. I was surprised at how quickly they'd arrived. We were in the downtown area of Sugar Creek, so they must have been nearby.

Onlookers stopped in their tracks. Others emerged from nearby shops, drawn to the chaotic scene unfolding before them. The cops's presence attracted attention as they moved toward the food truck.

Leesa gripped her hands, her nervousness palpable. "This isn't good."

"Of course not, but we can get with Sasha anytime to go over the menu." I said.

"No, no." Leesa shook her head. "I'm not worried about the reception menu. I'm concerned that someone might have seen Marcus walking over to the truck. Marcus and Darren got into a fight last week. They almost swung on each other."

My eyes widened. I started to turn and look at Marcus, but thought better of it. "So you think the cops might look at Marcus for this?"

Leesa sighed. "Or both of them. Sasha told me she had words with him too."

"Who is this guy?" I didn't think I'd ever seen him before, but of course, seeing someone laying on the ground with their eyes closed wasn't the best way to identify them.

"Darren. Darren Clark."

"Clark. I know some Clarks, but I'm not sure if I know that name."

"Well, from what Sasha told me, he'd gotten out of the food truck business. It's complicated but he started showing up about a month ago. They've been creeped out by it."

"I can imagine." When I saw the two people step out of another car that had pulled in behind the police car, I grabbed Leesa's arm. I knew Leesa was worried about her friends, but my concerns were for my daughter.

"This might get awkward in a few minutes."

Leesa turned, and I heard her suck in her breath.

It was Leesa's fiancé, Detective Chris Black.

And his partner. The small, but formidable, Detective Wilkes.

Chris still had his football player physique, but even he gave the more seasoned detective a wide berth. I'd had some run-ins with Wilkes. Mainly, she thought I stuck my nose in her cases.

And she would be correct. I liked to find out things for myself.

Wilkes's green eyes scanned the crowd assessing the situation. Thankfully, she didn't notice us.

But Chris's dark eyes flashed with surprise when he turned in our direction. His expression shifted seamlessly back into detective mode. He conferred briefly with Wilkes before striding over to us.

"Ms. Eugeena," he greeted me first, and I nodded.

"Hey, baby, you okay?" His eyes softened as he spoke to Leesa.

Leesa shook her head. "Not really. It's not every day you see a dead body in a food truck."

I sighed. "Chile, looks like lunch is cancelled for today."

Wilkes's voice rang out as she stepped up behind Chris. "Mrs. Patterson-Jones. Is this a coincidence that you're here?"

Before he stepped to the side, Chris gave us a look, warning us to behave.

Wilkes stood in front of us, her red hair flowing in the breeze. Her green eyes pierced us as if we did something wrong.

"Well, hello, Detective Wilkes." I said giving her my best smile. "Always good to see you on the case."

"Why are you here?" Detective Wilkes asked with a raised eyebrow.

"To get lunch," Leesa blurted. "Who doesn't want good barbecue?"

Chris coughed into his hands.

I ignored Chris and looked directly into Detective Wilkes's eyes. "I called 911. As my daughter stated, we're here to get lunch. Seemed mighty suspicious to have two barbecue trucks in the same vicinity."

Wilkes sighed. "I know I don't have to advise you, Ms. Eugeena, to let us handle the situation."

"Of course," I said.

We watched as Chris and Wilkes walked over to the other barbecue truck.

Leesa hissed beside me. "I wished Chris didn't have to work with her. She always comes into a situation suspicious of the wrong people. I'm sure *she* will give Marcus and Sasha trouble."

I turned to Leesa. "She would have to find some evidence, more than bad blood, between the two barbecue trucks. Just because people argue doesn't mean they commit murder."

Leesa nodded. "I know that and you know that, but suppose Wilkes focuses on Marcus and Sasha instead of finding the real killer."

I raised an eyebrow. "Detective Wilkes is good at what she does, and Chris has learned a lot from her. She will not arrest the wrong person for the crime."

But even as I said that, I'd seen how Wilkes barked up the wrong tree for a bit too long when she thought she had a person of interest. Leesa knew that firsthand from a few years ago when she came under Wilke's scrutiny.

"We have to make sure she doesn't ruin Marcus and Sasha," Leesa said. "This food truck has been their dream and they've been doing so well with their business."

I observed my daughter, the way she stood. I could see the wheels turning in her head. She had that determined glint in her eye, and I'd seen that look before.

In the mirror, when I stared at myself.

My motherly instincts rose. I needed to remind Leesa to tread carefully since this would already be awkward for Chris. But before I could say anything, I heard the most wretched scream I'd ever heard.

Without realizing it, I'd held my hands over my ears. A quick glance around at the horror on other people's faces told me I wasn't alone in trying to protect my ears.

Who was screaming like that? Was it someone who knew Darren?

Next to me, I heard Leesa groan deeply. "What is she doing here?"

#

I turned toward where Leesa was looking. Two police officers were attempting to restrain a woman from running toward the crime scene. She appeared to be Leesa's age and by the look on my daughter's face, she'd had encounters with the hysterical woman before.

"Do you know who she is?"

Leesa closed her eyes, as if trying to wipe the scene from her memory. "Yes. That's Jada Griffin."

"Is she related to the man?"

Leesa shook her head. "No, at least I don't think so. Last I heard, she was dating a man much older than her and she had a son with him. I'm wondering if those rumors were true and that person was Darren." Leesa scrunched her face. "Ewww, I don't see why though. He had to be like twenty years older."

I frowned. The woman was practically dragging both officers down on the ground as she openly grieved. Braids stuck out of a messy bun and her face was wet with tears.

"She looks your age. Was she in school with you?"

Leesa rolled her eyes. "Unfortunately, yes. We were in the same class."

I frowned. "So she's around twenty-six."

Leesa crossed her arms. "Mmmm. Darren Clark must have been her sugar daddy."

"Leesa Patterson!" Although I agreed, I didn't want my daughter to pick up too much of my bad habit of being judgmental. I felt like I'd come a long way, but we all still needed to work on our weaknesses.

My daughter shrugged. "It's true."

I felt bad watching this young woman carry on. "She must have had some feelings for Darren. No one wants to find out someone they cared about has died, especially inside his own food truck."

That part was bothering me, and the part of my brain that loved crime shows had kicked in and I was curious about not only how the man had died but when and who did it. The food truck had to be here when Marcus and Sasha arrived. Sasha said they'd worked this location every Friday the last few months. I wasn't a forensic expert, but I assumed someone had to have killed Darren before the Smokin' Ward pulled into their usual spot.

More outbursts interrupted my thoughts.

"Arrest them both." Jada screamed, pointing toward the Smokin' Ward truck. "I know they did it."

I whipped my head around as I watched Sasha tear away from the food truck. With her finger in the air, a red faced Sasha moved toward the other woman. "You better stop lying, Jada Griffin."

"Oh no, Mama!" Leesa said. "Can this get any worse? We got to do something."

I agreed. This was a crime scene and this kind of drama would have folks getting locked up even if they didn't kill the man.

Leesa sprinted over to Sasha with me close behind. When we reached her, I grabbed one arm and Leesa the other.

"Sasha, let's go back to the truck," I said, trying to calm Sasha down. "She's upset. Let's not make this worse."

That woman had the nerve to shout even louder, like she couldn't care less about making more of a scene.

And Sasha shouted right back. "You've always been a troublemaker, Jada. We didn't have anything to do with this, so you better watch your mouth."

Jada's face was a tight mass of anger. "Marcus threatened Darren. I heard him. You both probably plotted and schemed to get him out of your way. You won't get away with it. I'll make sure of it."

I caught sight of Detective Wilkes's annoyed face as she moved toward us.

I hissed at Sasha. "Stop it, young lady. You're going to make this worse on yourself. What's your girls supposed to do if you mess around and get you and Marcus arrested?"

The mention of her twin girls made Sasha pause mid-sentence. She looked at me, fear in her eyes at my comment. Then she looked at Leesa before dropping her head in shame.

"I don't understand what's happening." Sasha sobbed. "She's lying and slandering our names. Marcus and I worked hard to get this business going. This is our dream."

I patted her on the back. "It's okay, child. Let's go back to the food truck and you have a seat."

Leesa and I turned Sasha around, but behind us I could still hear Jada bad-mouthing the couple. I didn't know what that girl's problem was, but I hoped Detective Wilkes took care of it.

Leesa rubbed Sasha's back. "Don't pay any attention to her. You know she's always been a drama queen. If she cared about Darren, she would go somewhere and sit down so the police could do their jobs."

Her face wet with tears, Sasha shook her head. "I have never liked her. Some people never change. Jada was nothing but a bully in school. The other day when Darren showed up with his food truck, she was with him. They were two of a kind, hurling insults at us. We were minding our business, taking care of our customers. It felt like it did when we were in school. Adults should act like adults."

Unfortunately, a lot of adults were overgrown children. I started to ask more about the fight that Jada was shouting about when I caught a look at Marcus. Marcus was leaned up against the Smokin' Ward food truck. His eyes were glazed over, and his face appeared devoid of any emotion.

He looks lost. Is the poor man in shock?

I wondered why he hadn't stopped his wife from getting into an argument with the other woman. I turned to Sasha. "I'm so sorry this is happening to y'all. But I think you should check on your husband. Marcus is not looking too well."

Sasha's eyes zoned in on Marcus. "Oh, no! He doesn't deserve this. It's not fair. None of this is—"

She broke away from us and ran over to her husband, throwing her arms around him. The man accepted his wife's hug, but he still appeared shell-shocked.

It had grown quiet behind us. I turned to find Detective Wilkes talking to Jada, who stood, blotting her eyes with a tissue. By the way Wilkes kept glancing back in Marcus and Sasha's direction, I had a pretty good idea that Jada had continued her tirade, just a bit quieter. There was no telling what Jada was saying to Wilkes, but whatever it was, it couldn't be good. I prayed for the young couple.

I wasn't sure what we could do to help the couple. I believed they didn't have anything to do with the man's death, but neither Leesa nor I were good witnesses. The BBQ Fixin' food truck was in the parking lot by the time Marcus and Sasha arrived with their Smokin' Ward truck. The couple probably worked to get their truck open for lunch. The fact that Darren was across the street wouldn't have been a priority.

At least that's what I assumed. I wanted a chance to talk to the couple, but they were about to be accosted by Wilkes and Chris's questions.

Some movement caught my eye in the crowd that had gathered not too far from us. There were probably many folks like us who were looking forward to having a barbeque meal or sandwich for lunch today.

I squinted my eyes and shoved my bifocals closer up my nose. I had adopted the habit of letting my spectacles glide down my nose from my years of teaching.

There was a young man who stood taller than most in the crowd. He stood out to me not because of his height, but despite it being a warm spring day, he wore a hoodie. And unlike most of the onlookers who were looking across at the food truck, now surrounded by crime scene techs, the young man seemed fixated on Jada.

It could have been my vivid imagination. Or, maybe he was an admirer? Leesa speculated that Darren may have been Jada's sugar daddy, but could the young woman also be involved with this young man?

I nudged Leesa. "Do you see the tall young man in the crowd, the one wearing a hoodie? Do you know him?"

Leesa turned toward the crowd. I noticed her squinting. I'd been telling her she needed to go to the eye doctor, but my daughter could be vain sometimes and refused to entertain the idea of wearing glasses. I told her there was always contact lenses, even though they'd never been my thing.

Leesa's eyes appeared to finally locate the hooded figure, but she slowly shook her head. "No, I don't think so. At least I don't think I know him. I mean, he does look kind of familiar. Maybe we went to school together."

"Yes, he looks familiar to me, too." I taught so many students over the years, it's quite possible he'd been in my social studies class.

With my penchant for watching too many crime shows, I knew it was possible that a killer could lurk out in the open around a crime scene. It would be wrong to say the young man who caught my attention looked like a killer. That would be judgmental and pretty silly to assume by looking at someone.

There was a lot of blood around Darren, but I didn't venture close enough to gauge how he was killed. He could have fallen and hit his head. That could mean no one killed him. Or he could have been hit on the back of the head. Someone could have stabbed him or shot him. I hoped Chris would let us know, or maybe Leesa could pick his brain about those details later.

The young man suddenly turned in my direction, maybe he'd felt me staring. For an instance, his sad eyes met mine. He looked so familiar to me. This was definitely someone I'd seen before when he was much younger. But what was his name?

I could remember faces so well. But names, this old age and my memory would not always let me produce a name quickly.

I must have blinked as I tried to place him in my mind. Just like that, he'd disappeared into the crowd. I opened my mouth in surprise and blinked again. Then I scanned the crowd. He was there, and then the next minute he was gone. I knew he wasn't a figment of my imagination, Leesa had seen him too.

It was almost like he took off when he thought I could recognize him. But I didn't have a clue who he was.

Chapter 3

Wilkes took our statements, but Leesa nor I had much to add. We were the Greene's first customers and while we noticed the BBQ Fixin' truck first, no one had been around it. After all the chaos ensued, and with Marcus in shock, Sasha decided to close their truck for the day. Since we'd already placed our order, Sasha busied herself in the truck determined to send us away with food. From what Leesa got from Sasha, they'd arrived around eleven o'clock to set up. Darren's food truck was there and Sasha said they grumbled about it being parked near their usual spot, but they had too much to do.

As she drove back to my house, Leesa said. "They thought Darren would come over to bother them. That's what happened three days ago."

"You're referring to the fight Jada was accusing them of."

Leesa sighed. "It was more of an argument, and Sasha said that Darren started it. He came over and asked why they spent all that money on a new food truck. He said that they could have worked together."

I frowned. "Together? Where did he get that idea from?"

"Well, that's where things get complicated, and it might help if you talked to Marcus. But from what I've heard, there has been some beef between Marcus's family and Darren. Sasha said Marcus accused Darren of stealing his family's recipes and that it was a little too late for his business proposition."

"Oh no. This Darren sounds like he was a nasty character."

Leesa turned into the driveway and cut the engine. "I don't know why he had to bother Marcus and Sasha. I hated seeing that crime scene, but from what

Sasha has said, I think there were plenty of other people who were mad with Darren."

"Well, let's pray that Wilkes and Chris find those *other* people."

I still couldn't get the man's body lying inside his food truck out of my mind. I'd run up on disturbing scenes before and was hoping I didn't have to see anymore. My curiosity was slightly piqued by the circumstances, but my stomach growling kicked in.

The only thing that mattered now was getting food in my belly. Planning for Leesa and Chris's wedding was stressful enough. And I hated that our planning for the big event went awry today. Finding a dead body had placed a damper on what should have been a joyful afternoon.

"I'm so sorry about how things went today, Leesa," I said as we climbed out of her Toyota Sienna.

"Me too, Mama," Leesa said, reaching for some of the boxes. "I hope everything works out quickly for Sasha and Marcus."

"Me too, baby." I nodded my head in the direction of my neighbor's house. "Let's take Louise a few of these boxes. I promised her and Joss some barbecue."

After delivering the food, we entered the house to find Amos in his reclining chair. Porgy rose to his feet but stayed by Amos's side. Sometimes I felt like the two males in my household bonded better than I had bonded with the Corgi. The dog didn't always bounce up like he did when my grandkids came over.

I realized after the last visit to the vet that while Porgy still looked as cute as he could be, he had some age on him. Amos and I weren't the only seniors in the house. The pup probably had arthritis like his elderly parents.

With some effort, and quite a bit of grunts, Amos eased out of the chair. I was sure the smell of barbecue motivated him from his relaxed state.

"Let me help you all with those boxes." He sauntered over to me with his arms outstretched.

I gladly handed him mine. "I will be in the kitchen in a minute." I didn't realize until I came into the house that I needed a moment to myself. Old age wasn't kind to a sistah's bladder. We'd also been standing around that crime scene for too long. I started to head across the street to the Sugar Creek Café and use their facilities, which were always counted on to be clean. Knowing me, I would have also wanted coffee, and I'd had enough excitement for the day.

I took some time to wash my face and change into something more comfortable and appropriate for being back in the house – one of my favorite muumuus. When I arrived in the kitchen, the look on Amos's face told me Leesa had filled him in on what happened.

I reached for one of the kitchen table chairs and said. "I guess you've heard?"

"Yeah," Amos nodded in between spooning more barbecue into his mouth. "Leesa told me about the poor guy in the other food truck."

Leesa interjected with a weary sigh. "I wouldn't say he was a poor guy. I'm also not saying he deserved to be dead in his own truck either, but he wasn't the nicest person."

Amos frowned. "What do you know about him?"

A retired homicide detective, Amos still had an investigative spirit about him. It was one reason why I fell in love with him. And it didn't hurt that he was easy on the eyes, even in his early sixties.

"Let's eat first before we dive into all that ugliness." I didn't think I would have an appetite, but I was hungry before we left. Finding a crime scene and giving Detective Wilkes a statement left me famished. And that wasn't good for my blood sugar at all. We settled around the kitchen table, each of us with a box of barbecue.

"Mmm." Amos murmured as he savored the pulled pork. "This is good. I can see why your friends won an award for best barbecue. I guess competition was pretty stiff with that other guy's truck."

"Enough for him to park in the same place that Marcus and Sasha had already staked out." I turned to Leesa. "When they got into an argument three days ago, was that the first time Darren had done that?"

Leesa shook her head. "Sasha said he started showing up about a month ago. They thought nothing of it the first two times, but by the third time, it seemed weird. And Sasha was wondering how he even knew where to show up. Can you track someone like that?"

Amos raised an eyebrow. "There are all kinds of ways to track people, but I imagine if Marcus and Sasha posted their location on their social media accounts, that would have been the easiest way to track them."

Leesa slapped her head with her hand. "Of course. Sasha is always on Instagram posting photos from their locations each day. I need to tell her to turn that off. Well, it shouldn't matter now. Darren's … Well, he can't stalk them anymore."

I frowned. "Charleston is a big city. He could have taken that truck anywhere to make money. Why does this seem personal?"

Leesa shrugged. "I don't know. Like I said, Sasha has been freaked out, but Marcus was fed up. He's the nicest guy, and usually quiet. It's like Darren was goading him on purpose."

Amos commented. "Sounds like he was intentionally stirring up stuff. It would be good to know the background information on why. Did Darren think Marcus did something to him?"

Leesa shook her head. "I don't know what was in that man's head. I'm glad Chris is on the case. But I hope they let him stay on it. Even though he won't be able to tell me much, I want to be sure that he's the one investigating."

"Leesa, I'm glad you know Chris isn't obligated to share the case with you. He could get into trouble," Amos explained gently.

"I know. I know." Leesa moped. "He got stuck partnering with Detective Wilkes again. You know how she can be. I hope she doesn't cause trouble for Sasha and Marcus. I can't help worrying about them. What if they get blamed for something they didn't do?"

I reached across the table and patted her hand. "Let's take this one step at a time, baby girl."

"I know, Momma. Thanks for reassuring me." Leesa sighed and picked up a bag of leftover barbecue boxes. "I got to pick up the kids."

I felt grateful for Sasha stocking us all up with food. There was enough for Leesa to take some with her for

Chris and the kids. And Amos and I still had a box each for ourselves.

I followed Leesa to the front door. "Don't worry. And give Chris time to figure out what's going on. Like Amos said, he probably won't be able to tell you much."

Leesa nodded, but I could tell when baby girl wasn't happy. She wouldn't be able to help herself. She would bug her man. I hoped Chris understood her concern for her friends.

I gazed at Amos as he returned to his recliner. Porgy had plopped beside the chair, but the dog didn't look happy. I was sure his poor nose was filled with the scent of barbecue – none of which he could have.

Feeling quite full, I sank into the couch. "I can't help but worry about Leesa and Chris. With everything that's going on, I hope this situation won't put a strain on their relationship or wedding plans."

Amos raised an eyebrow. "Chris is a good man. This situation might test them, but it won't break them."

I nodded. I knew Amos was right, but I was still unable to shake the trepidation that had settled in the pit of my stomach. "I want them to be happy," I murmured.

"Then we'll do everything we can to support them." Amos replied. "That's all any of us can do."

I glanced over at Amos. I was certain the man could read my mind. I didn't exactly want to be involved, but I remembered watching Leesa and Sasha growing up. They were good friends for a long time until middle school. Like most girls, sometimes you go in a different direction when puberty hits. Then a few years ago, as young moms, Leesa re-established her friendship with Sasha.

I also knew my daughter had meticulously planned every inch of her upcoming nuptials. The last thing she wanted was anything to affect the catering, which she considered a vital part.

I had this familiar tingle, like an itch I couldn't physically scratch. Leesa had explained to us how Darren Clark purposely started trouble for sweet Sasha and her husband, Marcus. That sent my mind whirring in directions I knew it shouldn't be going.

MARINATED CONDITIONS

Usually when someone liked to stir up trouble, they made trouble in other places, too.

Darren, what did you do to wind up dead in your own food truck?

Chapter 4

Something about getting up at the crack of dawn to get children off to school and then having morning duty as a teacher broke any longing to lie in bed. And, despite being retired, I remained an early riser. Eight o'clock, even on a Saturday, was late for me to be in bed. But when the shrill ringing of my phone jolted me awake at only fifteen minutes 'til eight, I couldn't say I was happy.

I reached for my phone. My heart raced as I focused on the picture of my daughter's face. Something must be wrong. I fumbled with the answer button. "Leesa.

What's going on?" I croaked, my voice still thick with sleep.

"Mama, Sasha called me crying her eyes out. They took Marcus in for questioning last night, and he's still not home. She doesn't know what to do, and Chris won't answer my calls."

I sat straight up, making my head spin a little. "Marcus been at the police station all night? Why?"

Leesa wailed. "I don't know, but we need to help them, Mama. Marcus needs a lawyer."

"Of course." Anxiety squeezed my chest like a vise. This went downhill fast. I recalled the young woman, Jada, who was at the crime scene making a fuss. She must have gotten in Wilkes's ear.

I swung my legs out from under the cover and rubbed my eyes, which were still blurry from being woken up suddenly from my sleep. "Let me get the name of the lawyer Cedric found for Carmen a few years ago."

I headed across the hall feeling the drafty morning air wrap around my legs under my nightgown. I shivered as I made my way to Leesa's old bedroom, which served as part guestroom and part office space for myself. My grandkids stayed in the room when they spent the night, so I kept the office drawers locked.

As I fumbled with the key that I had inside the desk drawer, I could hear all kinds of noise going on in the background. "Are you still at home?"

Leesa responded. "Yes, I'm trying to get the kids some breakfast, and then I'm going to head over to Sasha's."

I'd finally stuck the key in the bottom drawer. It wouldn't have taken so long if I remembered to put my glasses on. That little keyhole was hard to see and difficult to open with one hand. Once my brain finally cleared, I had sense enough to lay the phone down on the desk and place it on speaker.

"Give me a few more minutes. That's good that you're going to Sasha's house. It's her and the twins, right?" Sasha had twin girls about two years after Leesa gave birth to Kisha.

Leesa said, "Her mother isn't much help these days. Well, not that she ever was, but I believe Marcus's mom is there."

"Ah ha! Here is his card."

Charles Barnaby.

The business card was a little worn since I seemed to pass along a lot of good business to this man. The last person I gave the man's name to was Joss, my next-door neighbor's granddaughter. The young lady was like a member of the family. It seemed to take little for good, ordinary people to find themselves in trouble with the police.

Leesa asked, "Mama, can you take a picture and send it?"

I cringed. It's not that I couldn't handle the task, but it was enough for me to find it. "Okay, give me a few minutes and I will send a photo of the card."

I definitely needed my glasses.

"Thanks, Mama."

After the call ended, I realized my pulse had been pounding in my ears.

"Lord Jesus, help that young man and his wife. Please lead Wilkes and Chris to the truth."

Back in the bedroom, with my bifocals fitted to my face, I found the photo app. With some effort, the dresser seemed like a good place to position my phone camera over the business card. Satisfied that I'd captured all the information, I tried to remember the best way to get the photo to Leesa.

Text it, Eugeena. One of your least favorite things to do.

Once I sent the text message, I waited. By the time Leesa responded with a thumbs up, I was ready to climb back in bed. With my good deed for the morning accomplished, it occurred to me there was no sign of the males in my house. Either Amos and Porgy were out in the backyard or they had taken off somewhere. I needed to let Amos know what was happening. But first, I headed into the bathroom to get myself together. I had a feeling the situation was only going to get worse.

By the time I heard Amos and Porgy come through the front door, I'd already prepared coffee, turkey bacon, and scrambled eggs. After eating, I'd grabbed my notebook and my MacBook. I figured I would busy myself with learning all I could about Darren Clark. The first logical place was where everybody posted their business.

Facebook, of course!

I scrolled through Darren's business Facebook page. The header for the page was a photo of the BBQ Fixin' food truck. Hard to believe Darren's body had been found inside yesterday. I could tell this photo must have been taken when the vehicle was new. Looking at this photo, I recalled how old and in need of a fresh coat of paint the BBQ Fixin' truck looked.

As I scrolled down the page, I saw tons of food truck promotions, but what caught my eye was how long ago the flyers had been posted. There may have been a reason the food truck appeared to need some care. Darren, or whoever managed the Facebook page, hadn't promoted the food truck for almost two years. I wondered if something happened to the business for him to neglect his business page.

My best friend, Rosemary Gladstone, often complained about social media and how they all wanted you to purchase ads. She'd recently retired from the hotel business and had started her own travel agency. Thanks to her, Amos and I had gone to Nashville last summer on our long-awaited honeymoon.

I had to dig around a bit more to find Darren Clark's personal page. There were a lot of Darren Clark profiles on Facebook. After refreshing my cup of coffee, I scrolled and scrolled some more. I'd finally struck gold when Amos arrived.

I heard Porgy come through the kitchen door first. Wherever the two had gone, the little dog was panting and thirsty. From the corner of my eye, I saw a light brown blur head toward the water bowl in the corner. A few seconds later, Amos approached me and planted a kiss on my cheek.

"Where did you two menfolk run off to this morning?"

Amos chuckled. "Porgy has a woman now, didn't you know?"

I frowned and turned my body around to stare at the senior dog, who noisily gobbled up the leftover kibble. "Sounds like this romantic meeting made him hungry."

"You should have seen him prancing around the lady dog as if trying to impress her." Amos poured a cup of coffee and took a slurp. Then he explained. "Joe recently adopted a rescue. Porgy and the lady mutt hit it off. Today, Joe wanted to talk about a new case that came his way, so I may be helping with that."

Amos often did work on the side with his old partner, Joe Douglas. Joe had started a private detective business when he retired. While Amos wasn't interested in the business aspects, he didn't mind helping out on a case.

"Good to know. I wasn't sure where you were, so I fixed breakfast." I shook my head. "Oh, and Leesa called. They apparently took Marcus in last night. Chris isn't saying anything to Leesa and her friend Sasha is frantic."

While I caught him up, Amos fixed a plate. He popped the plate of food into the microwave then turned to me. "They must have some type of evidence on Marcus if they held him overnight like that. Does he have a lawyer?"

"I passed along Charles Barnaby's number. You know firsthand that people who aren't guilty often think 'if I tell them the truth, they will believe me.'"

The microwave pinged.

Amos grabbed his steaming plate and pulled out a chair. "I will not deny it gets tricky when the suspect asks for a lawyer. I could try to see what I can find out without involving Chris."

I made a face. "Don't you think Wilkes might accuse him anyway if she finds out someone leaked information to you?"

Amos's shoulders slumped. "I was at CPD a long time, so it's not like I don't have other contacts. I'm glad Chris got the detective job, but it complicates things for him and us."

"Well, nothing says we can't do some good old-fashioned digging." I turned my MacBook slightly so Amos could see as he ate his food.

Amos shook his head. "I don't recall the last time I posted on my page. That stuff gets tiresome after a while. I like looking at stuff, but I doubt anyone would want to hear from me."

I shrugged. "I don't post unless something is going on in the family or if Pastor Jones needs us to promote something for the church."

My Facebook page had a variety of pictures that mainly included my grandkids, but also a few pics of me and Amos. When there was a bake sale at Missionary Baptist Church, I was the first to hound the young people to send me a graphic to post.

He peered over at the screen, his brows furrowed in concentration. "Find anything interesting?"

"Not really. I noticed someone had stopped posting on the BBQ Fixin' page about two years ago. Darren also stopped posting on his Facebook page about the same time. But he or someone posted on the business page two days ago for the first time in two years."

Amos raised an eyebrow. "What's the post?"

I frowned, trying to make sense of the post as I turned the MacBook around fully to show Amos. The post was a picture of Darren standing beside his food truck with his arms crossed. The caption read,

"Back in business! Better than ever. Come taste the difference."

Amos leaned in closer, his eyes narrowing as he analyzed the image. "Looks like he's trying to make a statement. Definitely a competitive guy."

"I agree." I zoomed in on the photo to study Darren's expression, as if I could read what was going on behind his stoic gaze. All I could see was someone who appeared determined, or something else. He was a handsome man with caramel skin and light brown eyes. But the smirk on the man's face bothered me. It almost marred his looks. I had a feeling Darren hadn't been a nice person.

Did he push someone over the edge?

Before I could think more about it, my phone pinged. I peered down to see Leesa had texted.

Marcus is home. Can you and Amos come over to their house?

I frowned. "Leesa said Marcus is home now, and she wants us to come over."

Amos pushed his plate to the side. "Why? It's probably best for Marcus to talk to the lawyer."

"Let me see what this child of mine wants from us."
I kind of already knew, but I needed Leesa to confirm.

Me: Did they call the lawyer? What do you need Amos and me to do?

Leesa: You need to hear their story. I think you both can help.

I sighed and showed Amos her reply. I saw this coming. I knew Leesa would want us to be involved. And I had a feeling if I didn't, my baby girl would try to investigate herself—putting herself directly at odds with her fiancé.

I couldn't have that happen. Not with a wedding in almost two months.

Chapter 5

A few years ago, a new housing development was built in Sugar Creek. I lived in the older, more historic neighborhood for most of my adult life, raising my family and teaching social studies at the nearby middle school. I couldn't help but admire this quaint, new neighborhood. The larger picturesque homes were painted in pastel colors and had perfectly manicured lawns.

When we pulled up to Marcus and Sasha's house, the first thing I saw was Leesa's minivan parked haphazardly in the driveway. I looked over at Amos. "My daughter is worrying me. I know how close she was to

Sasha when they were little girls. And I know having Sasha be a part of her wedding is important, but this is something else."

Amos sighed. "Sounds like Leesa is taking after her mama. She wants to help."

"I know, but her fiancé is on the case. She needs to trust Chris to investigate this. What does it say that we're getting involved?"

Amos swung the car door open. "Let's hear the story. I don't know Marcus or Sasha. The police questioned Marcus for a reason. Leesa may need to face the fact that her friends could be in trouble."

I heaved my body out of the car, feeling the weight of what we might learn behind those doors. After I knocked on the front door, my nervousness increased. I wasn't sure what Leesa had told her friends.

What did she think Amos and I could do?

The door swung open to reveal a short, round woman with soft features that immediately reminded me of Marcus. *She must be his mother*, I thought to myself. Despite the height difference between them, Marcus had inherited her facial features.

"You must be Eugeena and Amos. I'm Jackie Greene." She offered a smile that didn't quite reach her worried eyes.

"It's so good to meet you, Jackie," I said with a smile. "Thank you for having us."

Jackie clasped her hands together. "Please come in. We can use all the help we can get." She stepped aside to let us pass through the doorway.

As we followed Jackie further into the two story home, my eyes traveled up to a staircase on the right. There were portraits of Marcus and Sasha at their wedding, beaming at each other with pure joy etched on their faces. Various stages of the couple's twin daughters made up the other surrounding photos up the staircase.

The layout of the home reminded me of my own, but with a bit more modern features. This home was laid out in an open concept, which had become a popular design style over the years. We walked through the living room, which had a large flat screen television. An internet show that I'd become familiar with played quietly unwatched. My grandkids, Kisha and Tyric, often ran to me when they saw me. But today they were preoccupied and didn't notice Amos and me passing through.

In the room's corner, they were sitting on large bean bags across from the Greene twins. The twins, beautiful cocoa brown skinned girls, wore matching denim jumpers and pink plaid shirts. The girls's natural hair was pulled up into two afro puffs, one on each side. I was pleasantly pleased to see the girls having a tea party. Tyric didn't seem bothered that he was the only boy in the group.

Ahead of us was a bright dining room with a long mahogany table. Marcus, Sasha and Leesa sat in the dining room chairs. Someone had bought some Chinese food. There were white boxes strewn around the table.

"Momma. Amos. You made it." Leesa rose from her chair.

"Of course. We're here to help if we can." My eyes scanned the couple, who sat huddled at the end of the table. Despite being in their late twenties, Marcus and

Sasha looked like they both had aged since I saw them yesterday afternoon.

Sasha's auburn curls stood up, frizzed about her head as though she'd stuck her fingers in an electrical socket. More than likely, the poor woman had been pulling at her hair in frustration. She sat with her arms intertwined with her husband as if she had no plans of letting him out of her sight ever again.

Marcus's broad shoulders sagged like he bore the weight of the world. His beard appeared scruffier than it did yesterday.

"Marcus, how are you doing? I hope Mr. Barnaby will be able to help you."

He gave us a wan smile, the lack of joy clear in his glazed eyes. "Thanks, Ms. Eugeena. Mr. Barnaby was very helpful. The police were trying to keep me, but they have nothing on me."

Sasha choked out, tears brimming in her eyes. "I don't know what we'd do without you all and Leesa. That crazy Jada spewing all those accusations yesterday got that Detective Wilkes all on Marcus's case."

Leesa chimed in. "I don't get it. Jada has always had her issues. And we're not even going to go into why she was even with a man old enough to be her dad."

I patted Leesa's shoulder as I settled into a chair at the dining room table. Even though it was my first time here, the cozy décor and family photos adorning the walls made me feel at ease enough to launch into a question. "If you don't mind, can you share what happened between you and Darren?"

Marcus and Sasha glanced at each other. Sasha looked at us. "It's complicated."

I tossed a look at Amos. "Well, Amos is a retired homicide detective. I'm sure we can try to figure out what the police are looking for."

Amos added as he sat across from me at the table. "And maybe which direction they are going in. I can tell you from experience, the first suspect on their list usually remains the focus of the investigation. But I agree with Eugeena. Something serious must have happened for them to hold you for questioning for so long."

Marcus let out a deep sigh. "This all started about two years ago."

My ears perked up.

Two years ago.

That timeline matched what I'd seen on Darren's Facebook pages.

I leaned in to listen.

Chapter 6

"My older brother, Luke, partnered with Darren to purchase the BBQ Fixin' food truck." Marcus began. "Really, that food truck should have been solely owned by my brother. He put in most of the money and the work to get it going. Plus, he was the cook. Luke and Darren were friends since high school. Although, I never understood why they were friends."

I suggested. "Maybe Darren helped with the business end."

Marcus scoffed. "My brother was a BBQ maestro, and he knew how to work his magic on the grill. He didn't have a problem with handling his business. If anything, he felt sorry for Darren, who, in my book, has always been a loser."

Jackie broke in. "Be careful, Marcus. No need to talk bad about the man. He's dead now." She turned to us after admonishing her youngest son. "Luke learned from the best in our family. My husband and their father," she stated proudly.

Marcus grew quiet before he choked out. "I learned from my brother."

Sasha rubbed his shoulders.

I frowned. "I'm sorry to have to ask, but what happened between your brother and Darren?"

Marcus lifted his eyes. A sudden fierceness flashed back at me. "That's a good question. My brother died two years ago, and *that man* was responsible."

"Darren?" I sat back as though Marcus had punched me. This type of connection wasn't something I expected.

Amos also appeared shocked. He leaned in, "You think Darren caused your brother's death?"

Marcus nodded. "My brother was a good man. He was taken from us way too soon. No one knows why."

MARINATED CONDITIONS

The room had grown silent, with only the television playing behind us. I turned to see if the children were in our conversation, but they were no longer in the room.

Jackie stood. "I'll go check on the children, so Marcus can explain. I'm sorry, but this topic is never easy for me, even after all this time."

Jackie's eyes held unshed tears as she hurried away. The grief remained fresh for this family. I felt bad for them, but I wondered if this was the connection Wilkes had focused on.

Could they think Marcus sought revenge for his brother's death?

Sasha looked at her husband, who had his head bent. I could only see the top of his head, not his eyes. His deep voice rang out breaking the silence that had enveloped the room. "Luke was shot one night. He'd parked the BBQ Fixin' truck in a neighborhood known to have some problems, but it wasn't the first time he'd been there. The people welcomed them and enjoyed the food."

I exchanged a glance with Leesa and then Amos before asking, "Are you saying that Luke died near the food truck?"

While we didn't yet know the exact cause of Darren's death, the fact that Luke died near the BBQ Fixin' truck seemed an odd coincidence.

Sasha nodded. "Yes, he'd closed for the day and must have been heading home for the night. Someone shot him. No one in the neighborhood seemed to have heard anything or even ventured out to help. It was late at night. A neighbor who lived down the street always walked his dog early and found Luke by the side of the truck."

"I'm so sorry," I said. I shook my head trying to process this information. "Was it a robbery?"

Marcus looked at me. "No. They thought maybe it was a gang of kids. But the cash from the day was still in the money bag. No one entered the truck."

Amos asked, "So his case is still open?"

Marcus smirked. "If you mean not solved, yeah. We haven't heard any news on the case. I doubt the cops care anymore."

Amos spoke up. "So much happens that sometimes detectives have to focus on which cases have the most leads. That's a shame they couldn't provide closure. Do you know the detectives on the case?"

Marcus thought for a moment. "Mama still has his card. I don't remember the name, but he retired last year. I figured we would never find out. But last night, Detective Wilkes and..."

I felt Leesa stiffen next to me.

This is why I didn't want her getting so involved. This had to be awkward for her own fiancé to be a detective on the case.

Marcus sighed. "Mostly Wilkes kept bringing up Luke. She's trying to make it seem like I was getting revenge for my brother. That's a load of crap."

I had to ask. "What was Darren's reaction to losing his friend and partner?"

Marcus cleared his throat. "After Luke's death, Darren let the food truck business die. I don't know if he was grieving or if he just let it go because Luke was the heart and soul of the business. Probably the latter."

Sasha said. "We asked Darren about selling the BBQ Fixin' truck to us, but he refused. He wouldn't even answer our calls."

Sounded like some guilt to me.

"I see. So Darren never came forward to mention if someone had issues with Luke."

Marcus stated loudly, "No one had any beef with my brother. Luke was the one with the magic touch. Folks would come from all over to get a taste of his barbecue. He made the most savory ribs."

The young man had puffed up in anger, but he seemed to shrink into himself. He continued after a few moments as if he had to collect his emotions.

"If anyone had something to do with my brother getting shot, it was Darren. He always had shady people around. Darren is... was always looking for easy money. Most of it was spent gambling or on some risky venture."

Sasha threw her hands in the air. "He probably needed money. That's the only thing that explains why he suddenly got back into the food truck business. I don't know why he would sabotage us. We could have worked our businesses in separate locations. None of this makes sense."

I agreed. There were plenty of areas in Charleston for both food trucks to make money. So why was Darren harassing his deceased partner's younger brother and his wife? Surely competition between the food trucks didn't have to be that cutthroat.

I'd come here because Leesa asked us to come. I had to admit the more Marcus and Sasha revealed the family dynamics related to Darren, my curiosity had increased. I glanced across the dining room table and, based on the deepened lines etched across his forehead, showing his full concentration, I knew Amos was just as interested.

Amos asked. "Are you sure Darren didn't know who pulled the trigger on your brother? There had to be signs. Did Luke seem especially bothered by anything that day or the week leading up to his death?"

Sasha exchanged a glance with Marcus, a silent conversation passed between them. Marcus's eyes clouded. "Luke was himself. Always positive, always ready to get on the grill and start a new week of business. He loved feeding people. As for Darren, the police questioned him. He supposedly had an alibi. We never got a straight answer out of Darren, so if he knew who killed Luke, he took that secret to his grave."

Sasha gazed fiercely at us. "Since Darren held on to the BBQ Fixin' truck, we started our own food truck, the Smokin' Ward. You might say it was our way of keeping Luke's spirit going."

Marcus straightened in his chair, the lines of strain around his eyes smoothed out as he spoke. "I hoped we would all move forward in peace, but Darren started showing up about a month ago. Not with the food truck at first. It'd sat in his garage for almost two years. The first time we saw him, I thought he was coming to congratulate us on our success, but he was full of questions."

Amos asked. "What did he ask you?"

Marcus rubbed his beard. "He wanted to know if we were using Luke's secret recipes. Those were our family recipes, but he thought they belonged to BBQ Fixin'."

I repeated. "So, because Darren was a partner, he thought he had ownership of your family's recipes? That's pretty bold."

"Luke had quite a few signature dishes that he never shared with anyone." Marcus explained. "I didn't even know about them until he died. He left them for us in his will. After a lot of talking and planning, we used them in our food truck."

I shook my head. "I don't understand why Darren was irate about this even though he got out of the business."

Marcus crossed his arms. "Exactly! I reminded him that the food truck sat for two years catching dust. That we would have taken the BBQ Fixin' food truck off his hands, but he turned us down. He told us he would sue us for taking his business and the recipes."

Sasha finished where her husband left off. "It was so weird how he would show up at our location. It was like he was stalking us or trying to intimidate us."

He was a bully!

I shook my head, wondering how a good man like Luke got caught up with Darren as a partner.

Amos asked, "Did you post on social media where you were located?"

Both Marcus and Sasha's eyes widened as they realized how they were being tracked.

Sasha stuttered. "I didn't think about that. I post photos every day to encourage people to come out to the truck."

"It's okay, honey." I reassured her. "Social media is a tricky thing. Like you said, you want to get people to come out to the food truck."

I sat back pondering everything we'd heard. "You know what's bugging me? Y'all said Darren wouldn't give up the truck. He let it sit in his garage for two years." I looked around the table. "First, that sounds awfully spiteful. But I could be wrong. Maybe he missed Luke."

Marcus spat. "He didn't care about my brother. Darren didn't even have the decency to show up at the funeral."

"Oh." It felt like my eyebrows almost touched my hairline. "He didn't attend his business partner's funeral? What a strange man."

Leesa commented, "Maybe he felt guilty about something."

Amos added, "Hiding from something too."

I took a breath. "What had Darren been up to all this time? I peeked at his Facebook page. Did he just suddenly get back interested in cooking because y'all started your own food truck business?"

Marcus and Sasha nodded together.

Leesa asked, "Darren didn't cook, right? Who would he have gotten to help him cook?"

Marcus glanced at his wife before responding. "Darren couldn't cook to save his life, but he had some guy in the truck with him the day we argued. I've seen him before but I couldn't tell you his name."

Sasha pursed her lips. "I've never seen him before. He was older than Darren, I think. He had a white beard."

Amos spoke up. "Maybe Wilkes will look into him. Sounds to me like the new partner would be a logical suspect too."

"What about the girl who was starting all that ruckus yesterday at the crime scene? Jada. You said she was Darren's girlfriend?"

Sasha and Leesa exchanged a look. More like an eye roll between friends. It spoke volumes to me about how much they cared for Jada.

Sasha stated the woman's name as if it put a nasty taste in her mouth. "Jada has been with Darren a few years. They have a young son together. The rumor is that she was a side chick that ultimately broke up his marriage."

That didn't sound good. It also meant more people were involved.

Sasha jumped from the table like the whole topic made her antsy. "Jada was there three days ago with the little boy. She wasn't on the food truck, but she drove up. Her son looked like he was about two or three years old, but she had him slung over one of her hips. When Darren came over talking smack to us, she joined him with the little boy still on her hip. I told her she should take the little boy away, and she started yelling at me. A food truck is not a place for a young child. I don't even let our girls be inside our truck and they're way older."

Marcus shook his head like the memory pained him. "Between Jada and whoever Darren's new cook was, I'm sure they said an earful to the detectives. They kept questioning me about that same argument. Detective Wilkes wanted to know where I was the night before. I kept telling them I was here at the house. Both Sasha and my mama could vouch for me."

Amos nodded. "You have a tight alibi, but it's only family who can support it. Are there any other witnesses?"

Marcus shook his head.

"Well, we know you didn't do it. Do you mind telling us what Wilkes went in on you about? Was there something said in the heat of anger she's trying to use against you?"

Marcus held his head in his hand. "It was stupid. I meant nothing by it. Darren was taunting us about my brother's recipes as though he had a right to what's been in my family since before my dad was born."

We waited. I glanced at Amos who told me a long time ago it was best to respond with silence and let a person talk. It was an interrogation tactic police used a lot. I wanted to know what Marcus said to get him into hot water with Wilkes.

Finally, he looked at us. "I told Darren if he didn't stop being so hateful and disrespectful to my brother's memory, I was going to shut him up."

It felt like the whole room froze at the same time.

Amos spoke up first. "You openly threatened him."

Marcus threw up his hands. "I wasn't planning to kill him. I didn't kill him. After I said that, he moved on. He saw I meant business. Darren got in the food truck and left. I didn't see him anymore until I saw him..." Marcus took a breath. "I wanted him to leave us alone so we could run our business. That food truck has put food on our table and paid our bills. I did not kill him."

"We believe you." I glanced at Amos, who had a look on his face that didn't match what I said. Taking the cop side out of my hubby wasn't possible.

I decided it was time to try out another theory. "So, who stands to gain from Darren's death? Who gets that food truck now?"

Sasha glanced at Marcus, their eyes sharing another silent conversation before they turned back to meet mine.

"I don't know. Maybe LaShonda Clark, his ex-wife." Sasha said. "She might think she's entitled to something for Ace's sake."

"Ace?"

Sasha nodded. "He's Darren's oldest son."

"So Darren has two sons, one with his ex-wife and one with Jada."

Sasha pursed her lips. "There's no doubt Jada is going to want something. But they've never been married."

"But would either of them want the father of their child dead?" I mused out loud.

Seemed like the suspect list had grown.

Chapter 7

Amos and I talked throughout the night after we left the Greene's home. Where we may have gone out of curiosity, it was clear to both of us we were invested now. Before we left the driveway, Leesa asked us if we were going to help. I told her we would do what we could, but that she still needed to be careful and not alienate Chris. He had a job to do. I felt bad for Marcus that a statement said in anger got him hauled in for questioning by the police. That had to be a scary and harrowing experience.

The next morning, when I arrived at church, Leesa was there with Kisha and Tyric, but no Chris. That wasn't too unusual. Sometimes he went to church with his mother, Belinda Black. Belinda had been a widow for over a decade, and she depended on her only son to be there for her. Sometimes that was a source of contention for Leesa. But since the engagement, Belinda seemed to have come around a bit.

After church ended, I told Leesa I would see her at the house. Amos went to wait in the car while I talked to Pastor Jones about confirming the dates for vacation bible school. Being a teacher, the responsibility of planning this annual event always fell to me, which I enjoyed. A few years ago, we also received funding to offer an after-school program as well. Despite being retired, you couldn't take the teacher out of me.

This year's vacation bible school was a week before Leesa's wedding so I wouldn't be quite as involved as I had been in recent years. As I made my way toward the church parking lot, I thought I heard my name. When I spun around, I realized it was the twins, Annie Mae and Willie Mae. They often helped me with the children in the after-school program. And the way the two elderly women were approaching, I knew something else was up.

"Eugeena," Annie Mae called out. She was the more vocal of the twins, but today she needed time to catch her breath as she hurried over to me.

"Good morning, ladies. Are you okay, Annie Mae?" Her heavy breathing had me concerned.

Annie Mae wore a lavender hat that would have been more fashionable without the bobbing white feather on the side. "Did you hear about Darren Clark?" Annie Mae's chest was still heaving from effort.

Willie Mae sidled up next to her sister, her wandering eye unfocused as usual. She grabbed her sister's arm. "Annie Mae, calm down or you're going to give yourself an asthma attack."

Annie Mae gulped, shook her head, and then reached inside her purse. She pulled out a red and white inhaler.

I was so happy she had that pump. I was ready to call Amos over for help or call an ambulance.

Once Annie Mae got her breathing under control, she squeaked out. "Sorry, I know you know cause a little birdie told me you were there." She pointed.

I blinked. "I was there... Oh, you mean at the crime scene."

"Yes." Annie Mae said. She broke into a fit of coughing.

Willie Mae looked at me. Well, with her one good eye, she stared at me. "Do you think LaShonda and her boy are in danger too?"

I opened my mouth, but nothing came out. So I shut it. I shouldn't have been surprised that Annie Mae and Willie Mae would be on top of the latest developments here in Sugar Creek. They were the official gossip train. Sometimes they posed questions that made a person pause.

I hadn't given much thought to anyone else's safety. I thought back to the conversation yesterday with Marcus and Sasha. "Is LaShonda the ex-wife? Why would you think LaShonda and her son would be in danger?"

Annie Mae placed her hands on her hip. "Darren has always been trouble. Our sister never liked him."

I frowned. "Wait a minute. You're related to LaShonda?" It always seemed like the twins were related to everyone. They tried to convince me once that we were cousins, but I still didn't see how they came to that conclusion. Even my aunt Esther, who knew our family tree well, thought that relations weren't remotely possible.

"Let me show you," Willie Mae dug into her purse and fished out an iPhone. The twins were older than me by a few years, but neither one of them was interested in technology. At least that's what I'd assumed.

I watched in fascination as Willie Mae concentrated on the tiny screen. It was the first time I'd seen her wandering eye so focused. Her fingers danced across the screen. "Just learned how to use this thing," she said with a hint of pride in her voice.

Her sister shook her head disapprovingly at the device. "I still don't like those things. And everyone has them. No one wants to look in your face and talk. They'd rather text."

Willie Mae thrust the phone toward me, displaying a photo of a woman standing beside a tall young man with a tentative smile. Both were dressed in church clothes, but I didn't recognize the church in the background as Missionary Baptist.

"That's LaShonda, our niece," Willie Mae declared. "LaShonda's mother is our youngest sister from Momma's third walk down the aisle."

Third husband?

"Is that so?" I muttered. I knew the twins were the oldest and their mother had been married a second time when she had them. I never knew their mother was married three times. That had to be some family tree.

Which means they might be related to me after all?

I put that thought to the side and studied the picture. The young man caught my attention more so than the woman. I'd seen him before.

Was he a student of mine?

"Is this LaShonda and Darren's son?"

Willie Mae nodded, "Yes."

"He's tall. Did he play basketball?"

"Ace? Play basketball? No." Willie Mae answered. "He shot up tall after middle school, but he wasn't good at sports. Such a smart boy, Darren never treated that boy right."

"What makes you say that?"

"Ace was sharp as a tack," Willie Mae tucked her phone back into her purse. "That boy won the state spelling bee a few times when he was a little thing. This was before his big growth spurt."

Spelling bee. I was remembering the young man. His mother looked vaguely familiar too.

Annie Mae bobbed her head, making the feather in her hat swing wildly. "That's right. But Darren didn't appreciate those things about his son. He wanted a boy who was good at sports. Ace didn't have the coordination."

I frowned. "That's a shame. How's Ace doing now?"

Both the twins grew quiet for a few seconds. That kind of scared me because once these women started talking there was no stopping them. But I could see they were both fond of the young man.

Annie Mae sighed. "That boy had so much potential."

Her sister nodded in agreement, her face solemn. "Ace should have graduated from college and gone on to do something great like be a doctor, a lawyer or even an engineer."

I waited as a few lingering churchgoers waved in our direction. We all waved back.

"So Ace didn't pursue his education. That's a shame! What has he been doing?"

The twins exchanged a look that spoke volumes before Willie Mae sighed, her fingers fiddling with the cross dangling from her neck. "Well, Ace had his share of difficulties."

"Difficulties?" My eyebrows hitched up a notch.

"He lost his job a couple months back. But he's working with his mother. I don't think he's happy at all. I wished he would've stayed in school." Willie Mae added.

"Well, I'm really sorry to hear that. I hope he'll find his way soon." I didn't want to keep Amos waiting, but I was curious and knew the twins probably had answers. So, I asked. "Have you heard if there will be a wake or celebration of life for Darren? I would be interested in passing along my condolences to LaShonda and Ace."

Annie Mae perked up. "Actually, LaShonda is hosting family and friends at her house on Wednesday evening."

I tilted my head to make sure I'd heard correctly. "Isn't that unusual? Darren was her ex-husband, right?"

"LaShonda always had a soft spot for Darren... despite everything," Annie Mae explained. "Let's hope the *other woman* doesn't show up."

I raised an eyebrow. "You mean Darren's girlfriend Jada?"

Annie Mae and Willie Mae eyed me. "You know about her?"

"Yes, Jada went to school with Leesa, so I recently learned about her."

Annie Mae shook her head. "Then you already know. If that girl shows up, there will be fireworks. LaShonda calls her the home-wrecker."

Willie Mae nodded. "Darren was a knucklehead, but LaShonda loved him. He did some crazy things, almost had them lose their house at one time. But LaShonda stuck by him. That man having a baby with some young thing. Well, that was the last straw for her."

I asked, "How did Ace react to all of this?"

Willie Mae shook her head. "He was hurt. He's a bit of a mama's boy, so I'm sure he doesn't have fond feelings for that Jada woman."

I nodded, my mind going back to the crime scene. Three days had passed, and so much had happened, but I recalled the tall young man in the hoodie who seemed fixated on Jada. Now I knew that young man at the crime scene was Ace.

There were other people with motives to take Darren out. Could it have been a family member, possibly his own son?

It's always the ones closest that you have to watch.

Chapter 8

Sundays were my favorite day of the week. Worship and fellowship time at church were high on my list for the day, but I also appreciated family time. These days, even more than I did in the past. After widowhood and an empty nest, for a time, I only cooked on special occasions since my children were scattered to all parts of the Carolinas.

I hummed "Just a Closer Walk with Thee" as I set the dining room table. Something about the clink of the good china and the sizzle from the pots heating on the stove made me a happy woman. I didn't have as many settings around the table today. Cedric and his wife Carmen, both obstetricians, were tied up at the hospital delivering newborns.

I heard the front door open. By the sounds of little ones, I knew Leesa had arrived with Kisha and Tyric. Both kids came tearing into the dining room. Kisha chased Tyric who was wide open, holding something in his arm. I reached out and grabbed him.

"No running in the house, little man. What do you have in your hand?" I asked as I tickled my youngest grandson.

"He grabbed my purse, Grandma." Kisha stood with her arms folded, not looking too pleased at her brother.

"Okay, Tyric, give your sister back her purse and apologize. Gentleman don't run off with their sister's things."

"Sorry." Tyric said, handing his sister back her purse. He hugged her. Kisha rolled her eyes but hugged him back.

I winked at her. "You're a very good older sister. Who wants mac and cheese?"

Both kids raised their hands and voices.

"Y'all go wash your hands," I instructed. "I will bring out dinner shortly."

Leesa walked in, looking tired.

"You doing okay? Did you get any sleep last night?"

"A little, but Sasha called needing to talk." Leesa pulled out a chair and sat down. "She didn't want Marcus to know, but she was upset with him for saying what he said."

"Well, he was angry. Everyone says things sometimes they don't mean." I peered over at her. "Is Chris coming? I set a place for him."

Leesa sighed. "He said he was coming."

"Alright, well, sit tight." Normally, I would have Leesa helping me in the kitchen, but she looked down today, so I let her be.

I arranged an array of dishes that I knew my family loved. Because of my Type II diabetes diagnosis, I stayed away from my lifelong love of golden-fried chicken and instead opted for roasted chicken. I couldn't quite give up making my creamy macaroni and cheese with all of its cheesy, buttery goodness. I needed to splurge on something. I made sure I slow-cooked the collard greens with turkey instead of the fatback used by my ancestors. Even with the minor changes, it was soul food cooked with love.

By the time I set all the dishes on the table, Chris showed up. He'd followed Amos inside. First thing he did was bend down and kiss Leesa on the cheek. I watched her warm-up to him slightly, but I could tell she still had a bit of an attitude. Chris hugged the kids like he hadn't seen them in days, which may have been the case.

Amos led us in grace, and then we all dug in. Normally, it wasn't this quiet when more people occupied the table. But there was not a single word uttered. I glanced over at Amos, who seemed to have sensed some tension as well. Even Kisha and Tyric seemed extra well-behaved today.

I savored a bite of mac and cheese and eyed my daughter. Leesa's brows were furrowed. She was moving food around on her plate but hadn't lifted the fork to her mouth.

"Leesa, honey, is the meal not to your liking?" I asked.

"It's fine, Mama." Leesa shot a tight, sidelong glance at Chris before focusing on her plate again.

Chris shoveled a generous forkful of mac and cheese into his mouth. He chewed slowly and peered at Leesa briefly before looking away.

Oh no! This was what I feared would happen.

"Chris, you enjoying the meal?"

"It's good, Ms. Eugeena." Chris stated.

Leesa's eyes flickered with anger, and she set her fork down with more force than necessary. "Why did you have to question Marcus on Friday night?"

Chris closed his eyes and said through clenched teeth. "Wilkes got wind of the argument Marcus had with Darren, and she wanted to hold him. Believe me, it took all I had to convince her she had nothing on him."

I leaned back in my chair. "It would be nice to know if Darren fell and bumped his noggin. Then no one would have to be blamed."

Chris placed his fork down on his plate. "That would have been ideal, Ms. Eugeena. But he was definitely shot."

Leesa protested. "Marcus and Sasha don't even like guns. Marcus didn't deserve to be treated like some criminal."

"Leesa, I know I don't have to explain my position to you again. He wasn't under arrest." Chris looked over at Amos for help.

Amos cleared his throat. "Leesa, Chris is walking a tightrope here. He's got to do what's right by the book, even if it seems unfair."

Leesa's eyes flashed with defiance. "These are my friends. You've gotten to know them, too."

Chris's expression grew grave. "Detective Wilkes has already warned me. If she thinks I'm compromising the investigation, she won't hesitate to pull me off the case. I'm trying to not get thrown off so I can help."

I watched Leesa's shoulders droop, the weight of the situation was etched on her face. I felt bad for baby girl. This was not what she needed while planning a wedding with the man sitting across from her.

"Leesa, honey, help me clear away these dishes, will you?" I called out. Amos had taken Chris into the other room. The tension between them seemed to only get worse.

Leesa followed behind me, a stack of plates in her arms. No sooner had she set them by the sink before she turned to me with that same determined look she'd had since she was five. "Mama, what's the plan?" she asked, her eyes searching mine.

"Plan? What do you mean?" I scrubbed at a stubborn spot on a fork. I had a dishwasher, but there was something soothing about sticking my hands in a sink full of hot dish water.

"Come on, Mama. You were asking Marcus and Sasha all those questions yesterday," she pressed. "You and Amos can help them, right?"

"Marcus isn't under arrest, and they let him go. What makes you think that this isn't over?"

Leesa explained. "Marcus is a person of interest and you heard what Chris said. Someone shot Darren. Very similar M.O. to how Marcus's brother died."

"Look at you sounding like a future detective's wife." I looked at her pointedly.

She did at least look sheepish. "I know I'm being difficult. But Sasha and Marcus are my friends and they are helping make our big day special."

"And think how awkward this must feel for Chris, who wants to help, but also needs to do his job, and is marrying you in two months."

Leesa rubbed at a plate vigorously, making sure it was dry. "I know. I know. I'm not helping. I just have this feeling that this could get worse. None of this makes sense. Why did Darren refuse to sell the food truck to them years ago after Luke died? And why the sudden interest?"

I turned from the sink. "You're right. Darren's behavior made no sense. He must have had little respect for his partner to treat his younger brother and his wife like they'd stolen something from him." I thought for a minute. "They mentioned Darren was a gambler. I wonder if he started that food truck business back up because he needed the money."

Leesa's eyes brightened. "You think he owed someone money? But there was no way he could earn it fast enough, so they killed him."

I shook my head. "If they killed him, how would they get their money back? I don't disagree that he needed to suddenly make some money. I'm just not sure what it was for."

Leesa whirled the dish towel around. "So, what are you going to do?"

I snatched the dish towel out of Leesa's hand. "We're not cops, Leesa. There is only so much Amos can do. Remember, we can't get Chris in trouble."

Leesa's shoulders drooped again. She pulled out a chair from the kitchen table and sank down on it.

"But there is something we can do." I admitted, drying my hands on the dish towel. "Annie Mae and Wille Mae came up to me after church today. Guess who they're related to?"

"Those two old biddies?"

I smacked Leesa with the dish towel. "Watch who you calling old. They are not that much older than me."

Leesa giggled. "Sorry. Who are they related to?"

I still smarted from her statement, but was glad to see a smile back on her face. "LaShonda Clark. Darren's ex-wife. It might be worthwhile to have a conversation to see what LaShonda thought about Darren in his last days."

Leesa's eyes stretched wide. "Are you going to go over to her house just to ask her questions?"

"No, we're going to the celebration of life gathering. We will offer our condolences, then we're going to ask a few questions."

Leesa's expression brightened at the prospect of a new lead. "You think she will talk to us?"

I smiled. "There's only one way to find out, but first I'm going to need your help. One thing I know people won't usually refuse is food." I winked. "You're about to learn some tips from your mama on how to gather information."

Operation Food Truck Mystery was officially about to start.

The one gift I had was being able to talk to people.

Chapter 9

Sometimes I had to run from Annie Mae and Willie Mae, because, well, I could get into enough trouble on my own. But tonight, the twins delivered exactly what we needed. The only caveat was I had to pick them up and give them a ride. But walking behind them into LaShonda Clark's home felt pretty legit, as my daughter would say.

The April evening air offered a cool breeze. It had rained most of the day, so the ground was still wet as we walked up the curved path to LaShonda's house. LaShonda Clark lived in the wealthier part of Sugar Creek. The houses weren't necessarily newer, but they were well-maintained older homes that displayed old Charleston. Either LaShonda loved to be in the garden or she paid someone to keep her garden and lawn immaculate.

From the outside, if this was where Darren lived with his family, one could assume he had a good life here. Neither twin had anything good to say about the man, though they were determined to attend the celebration of life gathering hosted by his ex-wife.

It all felt rather strange, but Leesa was excited that we were doing something.

Annie Mae had chattered the whole time she was in the car. "I hope they like this red velvet cake. Sometimes I don't know what to bring to these occasions."

Willie Mae, who brought along a baked spaghetti casserole, had responded. "Me neither. I'm not even sure why LaShonda is having this at her house. Her and Darren hadn't been together in years."

I spoke up, hoping the women would cool their chatter before we got to the front door. "Maybe she's doing this for her son."

Both twins grunted at the same time. I peered at Leesa, who I could tell was trying hard to not burst into a fit of giggles. My children had always found the twins peculiar and didn't mind making fun of them, which I never condoned.

An older woman opened the door. I felt like I'd seen her before. With high cheekbones and wide eyes, she definitely was related to the twins.

"Isabella, how are you doing, girl?" Annie Mae exclaimed.

I found it almost funny they were calling this woman, probably in her sixties as well, girl. I knew she was their youngest sister, but Isabella appeared almost older. While the twins still dipped into hair color – jet black, Isabella wore a silver curly coif that I knew had to be the product of a good roller set. The gray pinstripe suit she wore had shoulder pads I hadn't seen since the eighties. Her eyes appeared owlish behind large eyeglass frames.

"Annie Mae. Willie Mae. So good to see you both. Come on in."

I could hear conversations spilling out the door. It almost sounded like a party inside as laughter floated out. I stepped up to the door to greet the woman known as Isabella.

"Hello, I'm Eugeena Patterson, and this is my daughter Leesa."

Isabella squinted. "Yes, I know you. You used to teach at the school."

I grinned. "Thirty years. Were you a teacher, too?"

"No, no. But I worked in the lunchroom for a long time. Had to give that up when my knees got bad. Come on in. LaShonda enjoys having people around her. She's in the kitchen if you want to speak to her."

"Thank you." The kitchen of anyone's home was my favorite place to be.

Once the door closed, warmth embraced me. I attributed it to having too many bodies in one room.

Were all of these people here for Darren?

From the conversation I had with Marcus and Sasha this past Saturday, I didn't have a good impression of the man. But maybe he wasn't that way with everyone.

Leesa commented softly in my ear. "There's a lot of people here. Where do we start?"

"First, let's get this food to the kitchen."

Leesa and I settled on making apple crumble pie. Since I drove us over, she carried in the bag. I heard Annie Mae's voice before I saw her as we made our way to what I hoped was the kitchen.

When we entered the large kitchen, my eyes fell on an elegantly dressed woman in the center. That must be LaShonda. She was a tall woman with a shapely figure, her long black hair cascaded down her back. As we approached further, the cobwebs on my memories cleared. I realized I knew her face. It was slimmer and younger than when I'd first met her years ago.

We waited as LaShonda hugged and talked to Annie Mae and then Willie Mae.

How did this beautiful woman end up with a rascal like Darren?

Despite the grief-stricken eyes, she seemed to brighten when she saw me. "Mrs. Eugeena Patterson. My goodness, I haven't seen you in years."

I smiled. "It has been a long time. You taught English for about a year at Sugar Creek Middle."

LaShonda nodded. "Yes. I thought I could handle teaching, but those middle school kids taught me a thing or two. I don't know if you remember, but you were so encouraging to me."

"Did you go somewhere else to teach?"

LaShonda chuckled. "No ma'am. I got a job at an insurance company the following school year and haven't looked back. I have my own insurance company now."

"That's wonderful! You have to do what's best for you." I clasped her hands in mine. "My condolences on your loss. I don't know if you know this, but my daughter," I turned to Leesa, who stepped up beside me. "Leesa and I were near the BBQ Fixin' food truck the other day. We called the police."

Leesa spoke up. "I wished I could have helped. I went over to give CPR."

LaShonda's smile faded. "Oh my. That must have been awful for both of you. I appreciate you coming. Darren ... bless his heart."

That phrase could be taken several ways, and I had a feeling LaShonda had a negative connotation to her 'bless his heart.'

Leesa glanced at me. "You know my friends Marcus and Sasha Greene didn't quite understand why Darren got back into the food truck business. He harassed them a good bit the last few weeks."

I have to say I was a bit impressed with how my daughter eased her way into a conversation about Darren within five minutes of being in the house. I looked at LaShonda wondering what her answer would be. For a minute, I was afraid she was going to balk at the conversation.

Instead, she sat in a nearby seat. "I'm sorry about Marcus. I heard the police were questioning him. That's not fair, especially after... the way his older brother died. I was as surprised as anyone that Darren finally took that food truck out of his garage. I told him back then to sell it to Marcus, but he refused."

"Well, after losing a partner like that, maybe Darren needed to grieve in his own way." I suggested.

LaShonda smirked. "Darren never cared about anyone but himself. Luke was too good to him, calling him a partner. I have always felt so bad about the whole thing."

"You mind if I ask why? Were things bad between Darren and Luke?"

LaShonda looked at both of us. Her mouth parted like she wanted to say something. "I didn't get along with my ex-husband, but I probably shouldn't talk bad about the dead. Besides, my son will be here soon, and this celebration is for him."

LaShonda knew something.

Was Darren responsible for his partner's death? LaShonda seemed like an honorable woman. I was sure she wouldn't have sat on information that would have helped the police find Luke's killer.

I changed tactics. Being around Amos all this time and listening to his stories, I knew if I kept going like I was interrogating the woman, that would defeat the purpose of gathering information. I was sure if she hadn't already ended up on Wilkes and Chris's list of people to interview, she would be soon.

In our Operation Food Truck Mystery, Leesa and I wanted to discover what had been marinating under the surface before Darren's untimely death. Anything to throw attention off Marcus.

"Do you have photos of your son? I had so many students over the years I feel like I should know him."

The smile returned to LaShonda's face. "Oh, he was definitely in your class. You were one of his favorite teachers. Come out in the hall. I can show you some photos."

Leesa and I followed her out into the hallway. My eyes fell on the childhood photos that lined the wall like so many homes. I recognized Darren, alive and much younger.

When I caught sight of the young boy with him, I snapped my fingers. "Ace Clark." I placed my finger next to my forehead as if that would push the memory to the front of my mind. "Oh my goodness, I'm getting old. I remember him now. He was small for his age, but the smartest young man I'd ever had. It was amazing how many facts he could retain."

LaShonda beamed. "That was my boy. He had an amazing growth spurt between his freshman and sophomore year. He got his height from my side of the family."

"Didn't he used to compete in spelling bees? In fact, Ace is his nickname, right?"

"Yes. Darren insisted he be a Junior." LaShonda grimaced. "But we started calling him Ace. He won the regional spelling bee championship two years in a row and won the state championship one year, too. He was crushed not winning the national championship, but he came in fifth place." LaShonda crossed her arms. "Those were good memories. Darren was even proud of him then."

I started to ask her if she'd seen Darren in the last few weeks, but we were interrupted by a gruff voice behind us. "LaShonda, how are you holding up?"

"I'm fine, Ray." LaShonda smiled as a broad-shouldered man stepped around us and sidled up to her. LaShonda had to be around five foot eight, but this man towered over her.

I stared up at him, but I didn't know him. "My goodness, you must have played football at some point in your life."

The dark-skinned man grinned. "I get that a lot. And you're right, I enjoyed being a linebacker many, many years ago. I'm an old man now, so all I feel are those knocks I used to take." The man held out a large hand. "I'm Ray Johnson."

"Nice to meet you, Ray," I replied, offering my hand. "I'm Eugeena, and this is my daughter, Leesa."

"Good to meet you both." He shook Leesa's hand.

Ray's eyes were on LaShonda when he asked. "How do you all know each other? There are so many people here I don't know."

I grinned. "I used to teach alongside this young lady when she was at the middle school."

Ray raised an eyebrow. "You taught school?"

LaShonda blushed. "It was one year. Ms. Eugeena here encouraged me so much, but I still couldn't hang. Those kids exhausted me."

"Wow, that's amazing. I never knew that about you." Ray placed his arm around LaShonda's waist.

They looked into each other's eyes so long, I felt my cheeks go warm, like maybe I was witnessing something I had no business. I caught Leesa's eye, and her eyebrow raised ever so slightly. The scene in front of us had grown awkward rather quickly.

We hadn't gotten as much information on Darren as I had wanted, but at least LaShonda and I had become acquainted again. Hopefully, it wouldn't seem odd to make a return visit.

I turned to Leesa to suggest that maybe we should head out, but loud voices bellowed from the front part of the house near the living room.

Behind me, I heard LaShonda suck in a sharp intake of breath. "I know she didn't show up at my house." The woman brushed past us like she forgot we'd been standing there talking to her.

Leesa whispered in my ear. "It's Jada."

I frowned. "Darren's girlfriend. Why would she come here?"

Thoughts of leaving were out of the question. How the ex-wife and the current girlfriend clashed was not to be missed. No greater time for people to act a fool than when someone died.

But somebody had killed Darren.

Were one of these women responsible?

Chapter 10

I had a split second of feeling guilty for wanting to get into these folks's business. Before I could say anything, Leesa had taken off ahead of me. My daughter had no intentions of missing the action. It didn't help that Leesa had harsh feelings toward Jada, which I still needed to find out more about.

Lord, forgive me, but I wanted to see these two women face off with each other too. LaShonda stated this get together was for her son, but I hadn't seen Ace yet. Why wouldn't Jada do something at her own house? Did she even share a house with the father of her baby? I had no idea about the living situation between Darren and Jada. But why would she come to the ex-wife's home?

Sounded like someone came to pick a fight. Wasn't that what Sasha said the young woman did days before Darren was killed? I also recalled both Sasha and Leesa mention the woman had always been a bully.

Yeah, she came over here with no good intentions.

There was quite a crowd by the time I made it to the living room. I shook my head when I caught sight of Annie Mae and Willie Mae elbowing each other in front of me.

Willie Mae hissed, "I can't see anything."

Annie Mae rolled her eyes. "Just listen. You don't have to see what's going on."

Like Willie Mae, I wanted to see. I moved up toward the middle of the hallway and somehow got a good look at what was happening between LaShonda and Jada.

LaShonda had her arms crossed over her chest, her face tense, and her lips in an ugly sneer. Despite her stance, she still looked pretty and more mature than her enemy.

Jada stood in front of her with her hands on her hips as if she belonged in the house. That girl looked a hot mess at the crime scene, but tonight she'd taken the time to wear what I assumed was a wig. Her face was made up with long eyelashes and bright red lipstick.

Who comes made up for a fight?

Neither one of these women appeared to be grieving Darren.

"What are you doing here, Jada?" LaShonda hissed.

Jada rolled her eyes. "I came to pay my respects to Darren. Is that a problem? Besides, Ace said I could come."

Darren's son was okay with this woman? Where was Ace?

LaShonda's nostrils flared as she took a step closer to Jada. "Really? Well, this is my house. Don't act like you actually cared about Darren. Your money flow is gone now, not that he ever had anything."

"What are you talking about? I loved Darren." Jada retorted. "We had something good together. It's not my fault that you strayed." Jada looked Ray up and down.

Oh, was there an affair between LaShonda and Ray?

Ray stepped forward. "Don't be making stuff up, Jada. If anyone messed up, it was Darren when he decided to have a sidepiece."

Jada snapped back. "Who you calling a sidepiece?"

LaShonda tilted her head. "No one called you anything, but if that's how you see yourself."

"I didn't come over here to be insulted."

"That's enough," a young manly voice rang out from behind me.

I sucked in a breath. I caught sight of the tall young man before I realized it was his voice. He wore a different hoodie tonight, but he was definitely at the crime scene the other day. Had he come to see his father?

Now that I saw his face fully, he didn't appear like the timid thirteen-year-old boy with glasses that recited many historical facts in my social studies class. Ace had indeed had a growth spurt after eighth grade. He had grown into a handsome young man. Out of all the people in the room, he looked like he'd been grieving the most. His eyes were bloodshot, and he could use a haircut and a shave.

He glided to the center of the room.

"Ray, apologize to Jada for what you said."

Ray's nostrils flared. "Boy, you will not tell me what to do. This woman is the one who came in here starting stuff."

Ace glared at Ray and his mother. "Dad loved her and she's the mother of my ... brother. She has a right to be here, too."

LaShonda's eyes narrowed at her son. "Really, Ace? I can't believe you. After all this woman has put us through, you just welcome her with open arms into my home. Sometimes you act just like *him*." She spun around on her heels and left.

Ace looked like his mama had slapped him. I assumed LaShonda was comparing her son to his father. Ace didn't appear to like the comparison. His desire to include his dad's girlfriend seemed curious, especially since he'd showed up at the crime scene with her too. Or did he? I'd been so distracted by Jada's tirade on Friday, I wasn't sure if they arrived together.

They weren't far off in age, but I couldn't see why Ace would take Jada's side over his mother's. There was a level of disrespect there, and I wondered if it might have to do with Ray's presence in his mom's life.

Ray glared at Ace for so long, I thought the two men would come to blows. Finally, Ray said, "I hope you know what you're doing." Then the large man headed in the direction where LaShonda exited. Ace stared at the man's retreating back with a look that could have killed, if that was possible.

I hadn't witnessed this much drama and awkwardness in a long time. As the crowd dispersed with whispers about the confrontation, Leesa sidled up next to me. "I can't believe what I saw."

"Me neither. But we're not finished yet."

Leesa eyed me. "What are you about to do? No one is going to want to talk now."

"Maybe not, but I'm going to pay my respects to Ace."

I walked over to where Ace stood, looking down at Jada.

There was definitely something going on between them. I would have thought Ace disliked Jada. But his eyes were soft, like he felt sorry for her. Like he had feelings for her? I hated to break up the curious moment. "Ace Clark, do you remember me?"

Ace whipped his head around. For a moment, I didn't think he remembered me at all, but then a sheepish smile spread across his face. "Of course, Mrs. Patterson. Wow, your social studies class seems so long ago."

Jada eyed me for a minute, but said nothing. Now that I saw this woman up close, there was something familiar about her.

"I remember you too. I didn't like social studies." She said flatly.

Before I had time to react, Jada turned to Ace and said, "I got to go. Thanks for inviting me."

Ace grabbed her arm gently. "You should get some food to take back home for you and Dougie."

Jada looked unsure of herself for the first time since she arrived. "I guess. It's not like we have nothing at home. I haven't been to the grocery store in weeks."

Ace told her, "Don't worry about it. I can pick up some stuff or we can do an Instacart."

Jada nodded, her eyes appeared downcast and if she would cry at any moment.

I was still stinging from her comment, unsure whether to be offended or not. I watched as the young woman walked off. I hoped she didn't run into LaShonda when she ventured into the kitchen. If Ace cared, he could have brought her some food.

"Sorry," Ace mumbled. "Jada meant nothing by what she said. She's been having a hard time...even before all of this."

"Nothing to be sorry for," I assured him. "You want everyone to get along, but death makes people act funny. I'm sorry about your dad."

He shrugged. "I used to think he never cared much about us. I'm not sure how to feel right now."

"You know I was there at the food truck. I saw what happened to him."

Ace's eyes widened. "Oh, I didn't know that."

"Was anything going on with your father? I understand he hadn't pulled out that food truck in quite a few years."

Ace gulped. "He lost interest after Luke died. I really miss him."

"Luke?" I asked.

Ace nodded. "He taught me a lot. I could talk to him better than my dad."

That was interesting.

"So when did your dad decide to start up the food truck? That had to be hard to do."

Ace looked off into the distance like he was thinking through some intense plan. "A few weeks ago, my dad found a cook. One weekend he had me come over to help clean up the food truck, and he was back in business that Monday."

"That sounds wonderful. Like a good bonding time between father and son."

Ace grimaced. "Not really. He didn't know what he was doing. I don't know why he didn't sell that truck years ago."

I sensed his discomfort and changed topics. I didn't want the poor boy to think I was interrogating him. "Ace, so what have you been up to? You were always so smart. You got your nickname from winning all those spelling bees."

He smiled. "Things change. I wasn't able to cut it at college, but I did a year or so. I'm working with my mom in her insurance business." His face fell. "I should probably talk to her. I didn't mean any harm. I try to be there for my younger brother; I never had a sibling."

I nodded. "You were an only child. That's understandable."

The sadness on his face disappeared, replaced by something else.

Anger.

"I'm sure Ray is putting things in her head."

Yep, he definitely doesn't like Ray.

Before the young man grew tired of me, I had one more question. Though it seemed odd, it felt like another lead.

"What's the name of the man your dad hired to cook on the truck?"

Surprised by my question, Ace frowned as if he had to think for a minute. "Rob. Rob Wallace."

I looked around. "Is he here?"

Ace glanced around and then shook his head. "No, I don't see him."

"Can he cook? I mean like Luke."

The young man shook his head. "He does alright. I don't think my dad could find anyone like Luke. Marcus already had his own food truck."

"So, you tasted the barbecue from the new cook?"

Ace gave me an odd look. "Why are you asking these questions?"

"My husband loves barbeque." Which was the absolute truth. "I like to keep tabs on the best BBQ in Charleston so I can surprise my hubby with some good food."

A wry grin spread across Ace's face. "Lucky man. I hope I can find someone to treat me like that one day. When Rob wasn't cooking for my dad, he carved canes. He can be found selling his canes at the Charleston Farmers Market on Saturdays." Ace's face grew solemn. "You know, the last time I saw Rob, he wasn't too happy with my dad."

Oh, is that so?

Rob Wallace sounded like someone I wanted to talk to.

Chapter 11

As I drove the twins home from LaShonda's, the silence in the car felt thick with unsaid words. None of us were quiet people, so the non-talking had me on edge. In the rearview mirror, I caught the twins giving each other looks and an occasional head nod. It was like they had their own secret conversation going. Next to me, Leesa fidgeted in the passenger seat. She looked at me, her eyebrows raised in a question.

"Is everyone okay?" I wasn't! The drama that played out between Darren's ex-wife and his girlfriend was like sitting down watching a soap opera. I loved talking to the television like the actors could hear me.

This felt like one of those occasions where I had to say something. But I wanted to know what the twins thought first. They were LaShonda's family.

Annie Mae stated, "I don't even know where to start. And, Eugeena, you know I'm not shy with my words."

"Well, I know what's on my mind," Willie Mae griped. "I can't believe that little heifer had the nerve to show up at LaShonda's house."

Annie Mae bobbed her head in agreement. "That's what I wanted to say, too. How did she think that would go? And had the nerve to pull Ace in there."

I looked in the mirror. "I thought it strange that Ace would invite her, but he seemed to be okay that she was there."

Annie Mae exclaimed. "Now he adores that little boy because Ace grew up as an only child. But he also likes to get under his mama's skin."

I frowned. "Why would he do that? I seem to recall him being a real mama's boy."

Willie Mae strained against her seatbelt. "Oh, he is. The reason he aggravates his mama is because he doesn't like Ray."

I thought about the big man and how he rushed past me and Leesa to get to LaShonda. "Ray Johnson. I've never seen him before. He's a very handsome man, but so was Darren. LaShonda had some good pickings."

I heard grunts from the backseat. I needed to keep my eye on the road instead of getting caught up with twins. I glanced at Leesa.

My child knew exactly what needed to be done. Leesa turned slightly in the seat to face the twins. "So how long has Ray been sweet on LaShonda?"

"Ooh child," Annie Mae waved her hands in the air. "Ray been in love with LaShonda since they were little kids."

"Mmmm," Willie Mae continued right where her sister stopped. "They dated in high school. Sweethearts until Ray left for the army."

I stopped at the red light. We were only a block away from the twins's home, and this conversation was getting good. "Let me guess, while Ray was away, LaShonda met Darren."

"That's right," both twins said at the same time.

"How long did Ray serve in the army?"

By the time I'd swung into the driveway of the twin's modest house, Annie Mae answered. "Ray had a long career in the military, but he probably wouldn't have stayed in as long if Darren hadn't snatched LaShonda away. He was heartbroken."

Willie Mae snorted. "But when Darren started mistreating LaShonda, Ray didn't hesitate to move in."

Annie Mae cackled. "You're right about that!"

I shifted into park and turned off the ignition. This conversation was getting juicier.

Leesa unfastened her seatbelt to turn around and face the twins. "Well, is what Jada said true? Who cheated on who? I wouldn't put it past Jada to be the sidechick."

Even though I'd parked in their driveway, neither twin seemed in a hurry to exit my car.

Annie Mae looked at her sister. Both of them looked solemn. Finally, Annie Mae spoke. "LaShonda is family and we will always support her. I believe she got stuck with Darren after she got pregnant with Ace. They didn't marry until Ace was almost two years old. Her and Darren were married for twenty years, but she put up with a lot from him for over twenty-three years. Let's just say Jada wasn't the first."

Wille Mae added, "But she was the first one Darren got pregnant."

I tried to recap what I had heard. "So, Ray swooped in to save LaShonda after she'd had enough of Darren."

"Something like that," Annie Mae agreed. "It's hard to keep forgiving a man when he done had a child with another woman."

"A much younger woman." Willie Mae shook her head.

"He was way too old for her." Leesa turned back around, her shoulders shuddering in disgust. "What in the world could Darren offer her?"

Annie Mae chuckled. "That's what everyone been saying. I don't know if you all ever met Darren before someone took him out. He wasn't a bad looking fellow, still looked young for his age."

"And he had good hair with pretty eyes. Real easy for women to fall for him." Willie Mae pointed out.

I wanted to get to who could have taken the man out. "Did you get a sense of who could have killed Darren?"

The car conversation quieted down after my question.

Annie Mae spoke up first. "You know LaShonda hated the way Darren treated her and Ace, but she still loved him. I couldn't imagine her killing him."

I thought back to the crime scene last week. Both Jada and Ace were there. Jada seemed so grief stricken, but tonight I wondered about her motives. And what was that about at the crime scene? Ace appeared and then disappeared into the crowd.

"Eugeena, thank you for giving us a ride over. This night turned out to be a bit more exciting than I expected." Annie Mae said as she opened the door.

"Thank you both for letting us tag along to pay our respect," I said to Annie Mae and Willie Mae as they climbed out of my vehicle.

While I waited until after the twins were safely inside their home, Leesa asked. "Mama, is this gossip going to get us any closer to catching Darren's killer? I'm afraid that Wilkes is going to come back to bother Marcus and Sasha again."

"Child," I sighed, turning on the engine, "I wish I could tell you it could help, but a lot of it is speculation. To dig deeper, we need to find out what happened. When I talked to Ace, he mentioned his dad had a new cook. Maybe this Rob fellow knows something."

Leesa sighed. "Leads. I heard Chris mention how important it is to have leads."

"And potential suspects. I think we have quite a list. We need to figure out motives and what happened with Darren the past few days. Somebody knows something."

I pulled in front of Leesa's house. Chris's black SUV was parked next to her minivan. "I see Chris had time to look in on the kids. Have you two been talking?"

Leesa sighed. "We try talking about everything but the case. I know I get extra sensitive about it. I wish this case was like any other case. Then I wouldn't have paid any attention."

"But Darren interfered with Marcus and Sasha."

Leesa nodded. "That's the part I don't get. Why couldn't he just start his food truck up again and leave them alone?"

"He certainly complicated matters." I commented. "I can't help but think his intimidation tactics were a cover for something else."

"Like what?" Leesa inquired.

"I'm not sure yet, but it sounded like Darren liked get-rich-quick schemes and money. He probably remembered how that food truck made him money back when Luke was alive. Anyhow," I patted Leesa on her legs, "you need to get in the house and tuck my grandkids into bed."

Leesa grinned. "You're right. They don't know how to act when Chris is around. For a tough guy, he's such a pushover with the kids."

"That's probably one of the many reasons you love him. Just don't forget that. I'm sure he's working hard to find the truth."

Leesa climbed out of the car, but before she closed the door, she bent down to look at me. "Thanks for letting me tag along. I know this is Chris's case, but it still helped me feel like I was doing something. I might find out some more information about Jada."

I narrowed my eyes. "Why are you so focused on her? She seemed like she was grieving for the man."

Leesa twisted her mouth. "Really, Mama? I'm sorry, but she didn't fool me. She might have been with Darren to get what she could from him, but I doubt she cared about him. Why show up to cause trouble tonight?"

I didn't have a response to that. The young woman could have just wanted the attention. "Be careful with your snooping. Kiss Kisha and Tyric goodnight for me. And I love you."

Leesa grinned. "Love you too, Mama."

I backed out of the driveway, feeling the weight of the long day on my shoulders. As I headed down the street toward my home, my mind thought back to all I'd learned.

Darren Clark had been a complicated man with a complicated life.

I sensed underneath the surface that danger also lurked around Darren. I couldn't quite see who would be mad enough to shoot Darren and leave him dying in his own food truck.

Would it be the same person who killed Marcus's brother two years ago? Did Darren die because he knew something, or was he responsible for his partner's death?

I didn't tell Leesa, she needed to stay out of hot water with Chris.

But I would reach out for even more conversations.

Amos had already retired to bed by the time I arrived home. He took one look at me and raised both of his eyebrows. With him being bald, his handsome face looked rather comical. I had to suppress the grin on my face while I removed the dress I had worn to LaShonda's home.

"Well, how was it? Amos inquired. "I can tell you are buzzing with some information."

"Give me one moment to wash up and get settled. There was so much to take in, but I'm not sure where it will lead."

In about fifteen minutes, I'd prepared myself for bed and climbed under the covers. Amos turned the television volume down in anticipation of our conversation. And I spilled everything. As I suspected, he had some things to say about the various relationships.

Amos crossed his arms. "Alright, so let me recap. You knew LaShonda from when she briefly taught school. Also, Ace, her and Darren's son, was one of your students. A real smart young fellow, but seems to have gone through some changes since he was thirteen and in your class. So, LaShonda didn't care for her ex-husband, but she had the celebration of life at her home for her son's benefit. So far, so good?"

I nodded. "Yes, she didn't appear to be grieving too much, but you know behind closed doors it could have been different."

"But she has a new man in her life. Ray?"

"Apparently LaShonda and Ray Johnson go way back. They were high school sweethearts, but the twins said he's been in love with her for as long as they could remember. When he went off to the army, Darren swooped in. I guess Ray hoped and waited for his time to come."

Amos smiled. "And it did. Darren messed up. But what I'm not understanding is this young woman who's Leesa's age. I'm with Leesa on that. Why the attraction to an older man?"

I scrunched my nose. "That I don't know, but I don't understand young people these days or their choices. I never could get a handle on my own children."

Amos chuckled. "You telling me. Your relationship with your kids has been better than mine with my girls."

Amos's oldest daughter still lived in Seattle. After years of estrangement, they'd begun talking regularly. His youngest daughter moved back to Charleston. Their relationship was much closer now, but Briana stayed on the road, getting back into the groove of her music career.

Amos continued. "We give them life and raise them, but they grow into their own person. Sometimes very different from us."

"True. I'm sure Leesa is going to do some more digging into Jada, even though I warned her to be careful." I sighed. "I'm sensing some strain between Leesa and Chris. They don't need this. The wedding should be more important."

Amos patted my shoulder. "Well, if Leesa's friends and caterer weren't involved, this would have been any other case for Chris. She's got your spirit for finding out things, Eugeena. I think all you can do is be there with her so she doesn't overdo it."

I cackled. "And you're going to back me up, you know how I can get into things."

"I have you all covered, babe!"

Babe!

My body tingled when he called me that. When Amos leaned over to kiss me, all my questions and worries were placed to the side.

I was retired. I could deal with that stuff tomorrow.

Chapter 12

Before Amos distracted me last night, I realized I forgot to tell him about a possible lead. Out of all the drama, Ace sharing the name of Darren's new cook seemed the most promising. But finding the man through my usual means was not turning up anything. There were a lot of results for Rob Wallace, and without knowing what the man looked like, social media wasn't much help.

A buzz from my phone broke into my thoughts. I glanced down to find a text message from Leesa.

Be there in 5.

I wasn't expecting Leesa. Usually I would have heard from her earlier in the day. She often called right after arriving at work and definitely during her lunch hour.

I'd returned to my futile social media search for Rob Wallace when I heard the front door and then tiny squealing voices. Leesa and my two sons all had keys from when I lived here alone as a widow. After Amos and I married, I never asked for the keys back. But the children respected me and Amos's privacy and would text me when they were coming to the house.

"Gramma!" Kisha and Tyric barreled into my favorite spot, the kitchen table. Their laughter was a balm for my soul. Being a grandmother was a whole new side of life. So different from the time spent raising my own children. Probably because I could spoil them and send them back home with their mommy.

My oldest son, Junior, lived in Greenville, and I only saw his kids during the holidays and on special occasions. I patiently waited on my middle boy Cedric and his wife, now married almost three years, to have children. I had a closer relationship with Leesa's children because I saw them practically every day.

I hugged and kissed my babies. Knowing they hadn't had dinner yet, I observed Leesa as she approached.

"You okay with a snack for these two? I haven't started any dinner for Amos and I yet."

Leesa waved her hand. "It's fine. I wanted to talk to you as soon as I could, and I didn't want to do it on the phone. You know... in case Chris came by later."

I raised an eyebrow. "You two talked today?" I knew when Leesa wasn't on the phone with me, she called Chris.

She looked away, her eyes focused on the kids. "Not today, but I'm sure we will connect later."

"That's good. Well, let me get these two a snack and you can share your info."

As I said the word snack, Porgy waddled in the kitchen. The sleepy-eyed Corgi sniffed around for whatever I was about to give the children. The old pup didn't have time to be too nosy before he was bombarded with rubs from the kids.

"Okay, you two, go wash your hands and no more touching Porgy until you finish your snack."

Kisha and Tyric raced toward the hallway bathroom. I kept a special bubble gum soap in there for them. Little Tyric could stand on the stepstool by himself to reach the sink. While the children washed up, Porgy laid down in the kitchen's corner near his food bowl, which still had some kibbles. Interest was apparent in his face as he eyed me pulling cups and plates out of the cabinet.

I shook my finger at him. "You have something to snack on in your bowl."

I placed chocolate chip cookies and milk in front of the two. As both little sets of hands dived into the plate of cookies, I looked up at their mom. "These have oatmeal in them, so they are a little healthy."

"Momma, they will be fine." Leesa snatched a few cookies herself and headed out of the kitchen.

I followed, keeping my ears tuned toward the kitchen in case a squabble occurred between the siblings. Kisha and Tyric's giggles from the kitchen table followed us out into the living room.

My glasses slid down my nose as I eyed my daughter. "So what do you have that's so pressing? And how did you do any investigating during your work hours?"

Leesa grinned. "I learned from the best. Nothing that a few phone calls couldn't handle. Besides, you know my boss moved me from the cubicle to my own office. It's like the size of a closet, but as long as I can close my door, I'm good."

I chuckled. "Okay, what you got and who were you calling?"

Leesa crashed on the couch and shoved her shoes off with her feet. "Well, I started with Sasha. You may have heard that we both didn't have the best time with Jada in school."

I sat down on the opposite end of the couch. "Sounded like she was your number one enemy. What did she do?"

Leesa munched on a cookie. "What didn't she do? Jada was the kind of bully that had ammunition."

I tilted my head. "Ammunition?"

"She found out things about people and used it against them later." Leesa explained.

"Oh, she sounds like a blackmailer."

"Exactly. Her being at the crime scene making all that ruckus was so uncalled for. Sasha said Jada was carrying on louder than Darren the day of the argument. Darren had no right to the recipes that belonged to the Greenes. She never was that bright in school, or at least she didn't apply herself, but according to Sasha, Jada was trying to sound like some lawyer."

"So, she thought Darren had a right to the recipes that belonged to Marcus's family?"

Leesa nodded her head. A deep ridge had formed across her forehead. "I'm telling you, Mama, things aren't adding up with her. She has to be up to something."

"It sounds like you are working on some theory. You don't think she shot Darren, the father of her baby? Then came back to the crime scene all upset like that." I shuddered. "That's plain evil."

"I have to agree. But something is up with her." Leesa leaned closer to me. "I called a few friends who were in high school with me."

"Leesa, you didn't?" I gave my daughter a look, knowing I shouldn't. She was sounding too much like me.

Leesa waved my concern away. "Mama! I wasn't obvious about my questions. I pretended to call about our high school reunion. The tenth anniversary is soon, and I got added to a Facebook group about it."

I chuckled. Me and my daughter were more alike than I ever realized. "Okay, so you used the high school reunion to get in touch with people. That's smart. But Jada doesn't strike me as a woman you want to get tangled up with."

Leesa nodded. "I asked people I trusted, people I knew wouldn't go back to Jada and tell her that I was asking about her."

"Okay," I said. "I hope so. Well, what did you find out?"

Leesa raised her eyebrow. "It could be a rumor, but I heard from a few sources that Jada's baby isn't Darren's son."

My mouth dropped open. "Oh, that's interesting." I thought back to last night, how Ace defended the woman being there. "Ace seemed to enjoy having a sibling."

"I know. But what if Darren found out that she'd lied to him? They could have argued and maybe got into it."

The thought horrified me. I placed my hands on my chest. "But where would she get the gun? She wouldn't be walking around with one being the mother of a young child."

Leesa shrugged. "Suppose they kept a gun on the food truck. You know, for protection."

I didn't think about that.

Then a thought occurred to me. "So Darren wasn't married to Jada, but if they were together long enough, it's possible he could have a will. That's if he thought to write one up. Amos made me do that a few years ago. You know when your father died, he hadn't done that. You just never know."

Leesa patted the couch cushion. "That's right. If she was in his will, he may have told her. Seems logical to put both his sons in his will."

Interesting theory. But was Darren really that thoughtful. I didn't know the man, but something made me think he only cared about himself.

I still had in the back of my mind that something else was going on here. It started when we talked to Marcus and he told us about his brother's death. The two deaths felt connected, but I wasn't sure where Jada fit in with Luke's death two years ago.

Leesa seemed determined to find something. Before I could express my concern about the path Leesa was heading down in her investigation, the sharp trill of her phone cut me off. She reached for it and smiled. "It's Chris."

I was glad that despite the tension between them, my future son-in-law could still put a smile on my daughter's face.

"Hey, Chris. Me and the kids are at Momma's."

I watched as Leesa's smile slowly morphed into an "o" as she listened to whatever Chris was telling her. "Wh—what?" Leesa's voice cracked, and her hand flew to her mouth. "Why? What are they looking for?"

This couldn't be good.

I leaned in a little and cocked my ear.

Leesa saw me and pressed the speaker icon on her phone. Chris's deep voice filled the room. "I can't get into all that, but I wanted you to hear it from me. Wilkes will knock on their door shortly with the search warrant. She's probably already arrived at Marcus and Sasha's house."

"Lord have mercy," I muttered.

Poor Marcus and Sasha. That food truck was their dream, and now...

Leesa stood from the couch. "Where are you?"

Chris sighed. "Wilkes made me sit this one out. She has me working on something else. I'm too close to this one, and she doesn't like it. I don't know if she's going to let me stay on the case or not. Look, I got to go. I wanted you to hear it from me first."

"Okay," Leesa said in a tiny voice. As soon as the call ended, she dropped the phone on the couch next to her and faced me. "Marcus and Sasha don't deserve to have this happen to them." She gasped and placed her hands on both sides of her cheek, her eyes widening.

"I hope the girls aren't there. Why would they search their home?"

I shook my head. "If Amos were here, he would have answers. My best guess is Wilkes must have found something connecting your friends to Darren. I'm sure it's a mistake." I offered, but I knew Wilkes was a good detective. The police could get things wrong sometimes, even Wilkes, despite her track record for closing cases.

"Maybe," Leesa stated, her voice void of emotion. "Chris didn't exactly say what they were searching for."

From my many years of watching crime shows, I had an inkling. I didn't want to say it out loud, but it was a real possibility they were searching for the murder weapon. But Leesa mentioned that Marcus and Sasha didn't like guns.

"Let's do what we can. Let's pray!" I held out my hand, and Leesa took it. Her hands were trembling. Mine probably were too.

We needed God to protect this young couple and their family.

Chapter 13

By late Friday evening, Leesa had already called me twice to report on how things had gone at Sasha and Marcus's home. They ended up going to a hotel for the night to make it a fun evening for their girls. Marcus's mom had gone back to her home. Before we ate dinner, Leesa called again.

"Wilkes is trying to put Chris off the case. That's not what I want. Mama, this is so complicated."

It certainly was a mess. I almost wished that maybe Chris wasn't involved. The tension between him and Leesa wasn't good. There had to be tension between the two couples as well, with Chris being the one assigned to the case. I prayed Wilkes switched partners so Chris could be put on a case that didn't affect his life so closely.

After I finished tidying up the kitchen, I joined Amos in the living room. He was reclined in his large leather chair, the tips of his fingers steepled together under his chin. He had spent the morning reaching out to one of his retired buddies, someone who could discreetly gather information related to the search warrant issued yesterday.

I sank down on the couch, feeling all the anxiety in my body melt a tad bit. This had not been an easy few days.

"I can't believe Wilkes thought Marcus would have the murder weapon in his home. Not that he did it, but surely he wouldn't bring it back home. And Leesa said he and Sasha didn't even like guns."

Amos sighed deeply. "Marcus may not like weapons now. I know when my girls were small, I took great care to keep my gun out of sight and locked up. But..."

My brow furrowed. "Oh no, I don't like when you use the word but. You're going to say something about Marcus that's going to blow up everything. Aren't you?"

"He hasn't been arrested. They're going to do some ballistic testing to see if the bullet that killed Darren was the same bullet from Marcus's gun?"

I sucked in a breath. "Marcus owns a gun."

Amos nodded, his eyes hooded with concern. "Marcus served in the Army for several years. He received extensive training in firearms and combat tactics. The man knows how to handle a gun effectively. Apparently, he kept his gun locked away at the top of the bedroom closest. But from what I heard, they took that gun from the home yesterday."

My heart sank. "They're going to check to see if it has been fired." I countered. "It probably hasn't been touched. And knowing how to handle a gun doesn't automatically make Marcus guilty of killing Darren. How was she able to get a search warrant?"

Amos took a swig of his sweet tea that had formed condensation around the glass. He swallowed. "Probably once Wilkes saw his background, and Marcus's military experience, that set her on the path. If he had a weapon, I'm sure it was registered."

Amos and I didn't talk much about it, but his old service weapon was locked away at the top of our closet. I wasn't against guns. My first husband made sure our two sons learned how to shoot.

My daddy loved his hunting rifle. He even called the gun Bessie. Or was that his car? Probably both. My daddy was obsessed with the name Bessie.

My mind was all over the place. I got like this when I was anxious. I could no longer sit still and rose from the couch, muttering under my breath. "Wilkes can't possibly think Marcus had anything to do with Darren's shooting!"

Amos watched me as I paced. "I think I know where Wilkes is going with this. There are a couple of reasons. Hear me out."

I didn't stop pacing. "I'm listening."

Amos pressed the button on the recliner so he sat up straight. He held up his hand and began sticking up fingers as he talked. "First, Marcus's brother's unsolved murder. Second, Darren holding on to the food truck that Luke purchased and thinking he has rights to the family's recipes. The fact that Darren would be so arrogant to claim ownership was because Luke let him be a partner. Eugeena, I'm not trying to play devil's advocate here, but that would have made anyone upset. Which brings me to a third possible reason in Wilkes's head. The detective can see the possibility of revenge playing out here. I would if I was her."

I shook my head. Sometimes I didn't like that Amos was a retired homicide detective. He made too much sense and in this case, I didn't need him to.

I placed my hands on my hips, my typical teacher's stance for scolding a student. "No. I don't believe it. Marcus and Sasha had already moved on with their own food truck business. Darren was the nuisance. Besides, I saw with my own eyes how Marcus reacted when he found the body. He was in shock. It didn't even register to him that Darren might have been dead even with the blood around the man's head."

Amos countered. "You said him and Sasha set up their truck without even checking on the BBQ Fixin' food truck."

"Yes, but three days prior, they got into it with the man. I would have ignored the truck across the street, too. They wanted to be at peace and just run their business. Maybe they thought he would go away."

I sat back down, tired from pacing. "What I want to know is what could have suddenly sparked Darren's interest in getting back in the food truck business after two years? What happened to Luke? What did Darren know about his partner's death? Those are the questions Wilkes should be asking."

Amos nodded thoughtfully. "That's a fair point. Which is why we need to find this Rob Wallace character, the new cook that Darren hired. He may know more about Darren's motives."

I raised both my hands. "Now that sounds like a plan. Leesa and Chris's wedding is two months away. The last thing any of us need is for our involvement in this case to cause any more stress. How do you propose we find the man? I'm sure Wilkes and Chris have to be looking for him."

Amos rubbed his stubby cheeks. He often shaved the white hair, but some days he let the stubble grow.

"Yeah, we need to proceed with caution. What other things did Ace say about the man besides he was a cook? Maybe he cooked someplace else, in other restaurants."

I thought back to my conversation with Ace. Ironically, I was talking to the young man as though I wanted to find a cook.

He can be found selling his canes at the Charleston Farmers Market on Saturdays.

"You know where we haven't been in a while."

Amos raised an eyebrow. "Where?

"The Charleston Farmers Market. Ace mentioned Rob might be there."

Amos tilted his head. "That could be a good place to start, but that food truck is going to be in evidence awhile longer."

"Ace said Rob had his own business selling canes. I guess he is some sort of woodcarver."

Amos rubbed his hands alongside the arms of the chair as if that would help him think better.

The motion had Porgy lifting his body from the floor where he'd been laying between us. The dog sensed our agitation. His eyes had moved back and forth the entire time I paced. He waddled over to Amos.

Amos scratched Porgy's head absently as he continued talking. "I'm worried about this plan now. Suppose the man doesn't want to be found. If he had some type of disagreement with Darren, he could be the killer. That would make questioning him an incredibly dangerous move on our part." He looked at me. "Maybe we should pass this information on to Chris. He and Wilkes are probably already on it."

I sighed. "Leesa will not be happy that we're doing nothing."

"But we're not. We came up with some theories and it was good that both of you visited the family. That gave us a sense of the other players involved. The goal is to get the attention off Marcus. I'm sure his gun is going to be cleared and Wilkes will eventually leave him alone."

"I'm praying she does."

Amos went back to watching television. Interesting enough, it was an old black and white western. I watched the men riding around on horseback, guns slung on their backsides.

My mind finally calmed down, probably because bedtime wasn't that far away. As my body relaxed, a plan sprang up inside my head.

Chapter 14

I hadn't been to the Charleston Farmers Market since last fall. Despite the early Saturday morning, many people bustled through the stalls. Even though spring officially entered the calendar a few weeks ago, the temperatures were already swinging up into the eighties. The air was filled with mingling scents of freshly baked bread, ripe fruits, and fragrant flowers.

Leesa and I decided last night to visit the market this morning as a part of Operation Food Truck Mystery. I warned her that we might not find this Rob Wallace fellow. To make sure we didn't spin our wheels, this

161

morning's adventure held some excitement for the children.

I held tightly to Kisha's hand as we navigated through the market. Kisha smiled and pointed as she soaked in all the colorful displays and eager vendors ready to sell us their wares. Behind us, Leesa and Tyric trailed along. They stopped now and then, with Leesa discouraging Tyric from reaching for things. The little boy was growing fast and had an insatiable curiosity, like his older sister.

A familiar voice called out to us. "Eugeena! Leesa! Over here!"

We turned to find Sasha waving us over. I didn't think to ask Leesa if the couple would be here. Steam rose from the porch on the back of the Smokin' Ward. While they weren't yet open for business, the barbecue aroma had enticed a small crowd to stop and examine the chalkboard menu in front of the truck.

Leesa beamed and shuffled past me to hug Sasha. "It's so good to see you both here. Are you doing okay," Leesa lowered her voice, but I still heard her ask, "after the other day?"

Sasha smiled, but the young woman's eyes appeared tired. "We're fine. The girls liked the mini-vacation we took at the hotel. But it's good to be back in the house. Bless Marcus's mom. She cleaned up the mess that had been made so the girls hardly noticed a thing."

I peered inside the window of the food truck, but I couldn't see Marcus. "Is Marcus cooking?"

Sasha peered back behind her. "Yes, he's in the zone getting the meat ready. I guess he's doing as fine as he can be. I can tell he's upset about everything, but I told him the police would see that it was all a mistake to focus on him."

Leesa asked, her voice low. "Did you know he had that ... you know, in the house?"

Sasha sighed and nodded. "I knew he had one, but he never took it out. It stayed locked up in the safe. If I'm honest, I forgot it was there."

"Well, once Wilkes gets all her lab results back, she's going to leave you all alone. Still, I wonder if they have any other leads."

Leesa griped. "If they do, Chris has been zilch on it. He thinks Wilkes is going to ask for him to be taken off the case."

Sasha reached for Leesa's hand. "I'm so sorry about all of this. Marcus said Chris tried to make sure he was okay, but there was only so much he could do. Wilkes was determined to hound him repeatedly about the argument with Darren."

"Speaking of that day, did you say that Darren's new cook was there?"

Sasha looked thoughtful. "Yeah, I'd never seen him before."

Leesa added, "He wasn't at the food truck when they found Darren, either."

I nodded. "That's what concerns me. We know his name is Rob Wallace. But he hasn't been an easy guy to track down."

Sasha's eyes grew wide. "You're thinking he did something to Darren?"

I shrugged. "It's a theory that we all have been tossing around. This Rob fellow had access to the truck. He would have had to be there to help Darren get things set up. We were at Darren's ex-wife's house on Wednesday evening, and he didn't show up."

Sasha crossed her arms. "Sounds like someone guilty to me. I hope they find him. We're tired of Marcus getting the blame for something he didn't do."

I patted Sasha's arm. "God will make sure everything works out. Don't you worry."

Marcus showed up while we were talking and poked his head through the food truck window. "Hey, ladies. Good to see you. We will be open at eleven o'clock if you want an early lunch."

"That sounds good." I said.

Sasha peered up at her husband, concern still on her face. "Honey, do you know Rob Wallace, the guy who was cooking for Darren? He was there that day Darren was arguing with us."

Marcus grimaced. "I was trying to put all thoughts of Darren out of my head. But, yeah, I kind of remember an older dude with him. He was bald with a white beard."

"Ms. Eugeena and Leesa think he may know something about what happened to Darren." Sasha gushed.

"It's a theory," I stated turning to Marcus. "Since Darren and Luke grew up together, do you recall seeing Rob before?"

Marcus had been wiping down the counter in front of him. "He looked familiar to me. But I don't know where I've seen him before."

"Don't worry about it. I'm sure the police are on the same track as we are. The man is bound to show up somewhere."

We said goodbye to the Greenes and walked around the market some more. When we rounded a corner, a row of booths was laid out in front of us. We'd entered the craft section. Quilts, sweetgrass baskets, dolls, pretty much any product that had been spun by someone's hands, lay in front of us.

We stopped in front of a booth.

Sarah's Lowcountry Woven Treasures.

Kisha had a fascination with sweetgrass baskets and pulled me toward the dark-skinned woman sitting in a wicker rocking chair. The woman grinned. "Gud mornin, chile," she said.

I recognized the Geechee accent and smiled.

"Are you Sarah?" I pointed to the sign.

The woman let out a deep-throated laugh. "Dat be me. Yes, ma'am. Let me know if you want anything."

I stood with Kisha, watching in fascination as the woman's hands moved in rhythm, crafting the long sweetgrass into a pattern. Not too far away, I heard a deep male voice break into song. It was a familiar hymn that was sung in the style that melded southern and ancestral West African roots together.

"Swing low, sweet chariot, comin' fuh tuh carry me home. Swing low, sweet chariot, comin' fuh tuh carry me home."

"Who's singing?" I asked. "His voice is so majestic."

The sweetgrass basket maker smiled. "That's Rob. People used to him."

Rob. Rob Wallace!

I turned to see if I could catch sight of the singer. My eyes found him and my stomach lurched with a start.

The man had his head thrown back, and he rocked as he sang. He was bald with a white beard. I looked at his booth. Intricately carved canes and walking sticks hung in rows beside him.

Then I recalled again what Ace said.

He can be found selling his canes.

That had to be him. But he was out in the open. Maybe we were wrong, and the man had nothing to hide. Behind me, I could hear Leesa fussing at Tyric. He'd grown tired of walking and the crowds. We probably needed to take the kids to get a snack.

I went over to Leesa and whispered. "I think I found Rob Wallace."

"Where?" she whipped her head around, spinning in different directions.

"Keep your cool. I believe he's the singing man over at the booth with all the canes. We should probably get the kids something to eat and think of a strategy."

Leesa's eyes grew wide. "Look who else is here?"

I followed her gaze back to the booth. I hadn't realized the man had stopped singing. He now stood in a face-off with a familiar face—Jada.

I couldn't hear what they were saying, but Jada's angry voice rose, and I heard the last part of her comments to Rob.

"... all your fault," Jada pointed.

Was Jada suspicious of Rob's involvement in Darren's murder?

Chapter 15

I grabbed Leesa's arm. "We should wait for her to leave. Since she knows you, I don't want her to connect the dots. She had to have seen us at the crime scene or at LaShonda's house."

Leesa griped. "It's not like we're stalking her. What do you think she's talking to him about?"

I turned my body so I could peer over with a sideways glance. "I don't know, but he doesn't look pleased to see her." We watched for a few moments. Rob grabbed a nearby cane.

Leesa picked up Tyric into her arms. "Oh no, what's happening? Is he about to hit her with the cane?"

Amos's warnings were in my head. This man could be dangerous. I grabbed Kisha, who had a look of concern on her face. "Turn this way, Kisha."

But the man didn't resort to violence. Instead, he shook the cane at Jada.

"Get away from me," he shouted. "I wish that man never contacted me. He was a no good scoundrel looking for easy money. No such thing! He got what was coming to him."

Jada stepped back and shoved her middle finger in the air at the man. "Some kind of friend you turned out to be!" When she spun around, her face was a mass of fury.

"Oh, let's turn. She's about to stomp over in this direction."

We waited until Jada stormed past us.

Leesa let out a sigh. "At least she went in the opposite direction. The last thing Sasha and Marcus need is to see *her*. But I wonder what that was all about."

"I don't know, but I want to check out those canes a little closer. I think you should get the kids a snack."

Leesa's eyes grew wide. "Mama, I'm not leaving you to talk to that man alone."

"Leesa, all these people are around and I would rather not have the man around the ..." I didn't look in her direction, I knew Kisha was probably all in our conversation. I subtly tilted my head toward the little girl soaking up grown folks's business.

Thankfully, Leesa caught the hint. "Okay, we're going to head back to the Smokin' Ward food truck. I expect to see you in ten minutes."

"It might be fifteen."

Leesa rolled her eyes. "Fifteen minutes or I'm going to send Marcus to get you."

With Kisha on one side and Tyric on the other, I watched Leesa march away and settled my nerves with a prayer. I didn't know if I was getting ready to talk to Darren's killer or not, but I certainly didn't want to be on the other end of a cane upside my head.

I walked over and browsed the display. Above the canes was a sign.

Gullah Canes & Sticks

Rob didn't look up at me. I saw why. He was talking animatedly on the phone with somebody, his face taut with anger. I cocked my ear so I could hear, but I only heard one-sided snatches of the conversation.

"She's crazy...trying to blame me. Like I got him into something. I told that man I didn't want nothing to do with that nonsense. I served my time and I wanted no trouble in my life. If he decided to get into something illegal, I told him I was out. I was only there to cook."

I reached out and touched a beautiful mahogany walking stick, running my fingers along the smooth surface. It was adorned with an intricate carving of an elephant's head. If this was the man's work, he was extremely talented. Most of the sticker prices were over a $100, so I imagined he made good money.

"May I help you?" A toothy smile replaced the scowl from a moment ago. The man had a surprisingly gleaming smile, but I imagined the white teeth could have been veneers or dentures.

"These are beautiful," I commented. "My Aunt Esther would love something like this. Do you have any others with elephants?" I hadn't intended to buy anything from the market other than fresh vegetables and fruit, but this caught my eye. My aunt despised being in a wheelchair. On occasion, I'm sure she would love the walking stick as an option if she didn't have too far to walk. She also loved elephants.

"I sure do." He reached behind him and pulled out two other canes. "Such a majestic animal. I enjoyed carving these. You see how I carved each of the trunks different?"

I studied the other ones. "You carved all of these yourself?"

He smiled. "Yes, ma'am. I craft each of these from what I can find in the woods, sometimes oak, other times cypress. These all take months, but I enjoy it. Learned woodcarving from my daddy. He learned from his."

This conversation reminded me of the one I had earlier with Marcus about how he and Luke learned to cook barbecue from their father. Even in my case, my son Cedric followed in his dad's footsteps and became an obstetrician.

"You are so talented. I'm glad you were suggested to me."

Rob eyed me warily. "Oh, who recommended my work?"

I seized the opportunity, but I didn't want to throw Ace under the bus. "I can't remember, but I was at the home of a friend. Her ex-husband had been killed last week. She mentioned how he was starting a food truck business. Your name came up as the cook."

Rob's expression hardened, and for a moment, I thought he would shake his cane at me like he did at Jada. But then, something in his demeanor shifted, and he let out a weary sigh.

"You must be talking about Darren Clark. Yeah, I helped him cook barbeque for a few weeks." Rob admitted gruffly. "I do like to cook, so I figured the extra cash from the food truck wouldn't hurt. I've worked in restaurants all my life and this was a new venture."

"Will you continue the business? Looks like you do well with these canes."

Rob's gaze flitted around the market, as if checking for eavesdroppers. "To tell the truth, I would rather do the wood carving. More peaceful. The whole food truck thing made me nervous. Darren had a former partner who'd been killed a few years ago. Then he got killed too. Something must be cursed about that truck!"

Or Darren could have been up to something illegal. At least that's what I picked up on from eavesdropping on his phone conversation.

I shook my head. "I don't know if the truck is cursed. Darren sounded like an awful man. He didn't treat his wife... well ex-wife very well."

Rob pursed his lips in disgust. "Like I said, I only cooked a few weeks for him. I kind of got fed up..." He paused like he was going to say more. Finally he said, "He was more trouble than I bargained for."

So Rob had already stopped working for Darren. What exactly was Darren going to do without a cook? There was no way he could keep the food truck going.

"His poor kids. I taught his oldest son when he was younger. I was a social studies teacher for a really long time."

"Wow." Rob grinned. "So you're retired now. I know you're glad. Teaching is hard now-a-days."

"Yes, sir, it is. Hard for the kids, too. I hope those two boys will be okay."

Rob waved his hand. "His oldest, Ace, will be fine. His mother is a good woman. I think Darren's ex must've still had a soft spot for him. She gave him money. Poor woman."

I stretched my eyes in real surprise. "She gave her ex-husband money. You know, I was surprised she had the celebration of life gathering at her house. It seemed like she'd moved on with a new man and everything."

Rob shrugged. "I don't know what the deal was, but she came by the truck a few days ago. I caught her handing Darren an envelope. He took it and looked inside. Even though I was a few feet away, I could tell there was a lot of cash."

Seemed like a bad idea.

I had questions.

LaShonda appeared to be doing well for herself, running her own insurance business and having a fabulous home. It was rumored that Darren liked get-rich-quick schemes. Could LaShonda have gotten caught up as well? Was this why she put up with her ex-husband's philandering? Could the fabulous home and insurance company have been obtained by less than legal means?

My trip to the farmers market only generated more questions. I didn't want it to seem like I'd wasted Rob's time, so I said, "Let me get the walking stick right there. Do you take credit cards?" It was a splurge item on my fixed income, but I felt like it was worth the effort.

As Rob processed my payment, I thought back to being at LaShonda's house last week. Talking to LaShonda again would be in my future. She didn't seem like she cared for Darren anymore. But according to what Rob told me, her words didn't match her actions.

But what if Darren had something on LaShonda?

Could he have been blackmailing her?

Now that was a good reason to get rid of someone.

Rob handed me back my card. As I reached to take it from his hand, he seemed to freeze. His eyes were looking behind me. I had that prickly feeling when someone's eyes were on your back. I turned around, thinking maybe I'd gone over my fifteen minutes and Leesa had sent Marcus.

Nope. Detective Wilkes stood behind me with her arms crossed.

What in the world was she doing here?

Chapter 16

I wasn't expecting to see Detective Wilkes at the farmers market, but I tried to play it cool. I turned around and took the wrapped cane and my receipt from Rob. My purchase had been genuine, but I had some questions for Rob that still needed answers. Now it appeared I wouldn't be able to ask them. I was relieved I'd sent Leesa and the kids back to the Smokin' Ward truck, but I wondered if Wilkes was here to bother Marcus again.

"Thank you for your beautiful work, sir. I know my aunt is going to love it."

Rob smiled, but his smile didn't extend to his eyes. He warily watched Wilkes. I couldn't blame him. Between her crisp white shirt, stiff blazer and bun, she looked like a cop. Her badge also peeked out from under her blazer, catching the sunlight. I was sure she had a holster slung across her shoulder.

I stepped away from Rob's booth, hoping the detective would let me walk away. "It's good to see you," I said, hoping my voice sounded casual.

Wilkes gave me a nod, but I could tell she was monitoring Rob. "I see you are out and about on a Saturday. I hope you are not getting into any trouble?" she asked, her tone light but probing.

"Of course not. Just getting a few things." I replied, holding up the cane. "This beauty is for my Aunt Esther."

Wilkes glanced at the walking stick in my hand. "That is some good craftmanship there."

The small talk made my right eye twitch. I sensed something was about to go down. Wilke's presence must have struck fear in Rob. In a flash, he'd disappeared around the back of the booth.

Don't run!

I cringed and moved back as Wilkes took off after Rob. She must have had a few deputies with her because two men passed by me following behind her.

I stood with my mouth open, not sure what to do. When I glanced around, I saw other people had also stopped, enthralled by the chase. The woman who'd been crafting a sweetgrass basket dropped it.

She came toward me. "What happened to Rob?"

"You know him well?" I asked.

The woman rolled her eyes. "I've known him all my life. He is my older brutha, but I tink I act more like the oldest."

Now that I looked closer at the woman, I could see the resemblance around the eyes and nose. The woman had a deeper Geechee accent than her brother. "Why would the police want him?"

The woman rolled her eyes. "I tole dat man to not mess with that Darren fello. He's a bad man. Rob worked hard to make his life guud. He'd come back here after bein' away so long."

"He told me he was cooking for the man who was killed last week in the food truck." I said. "Maybe the police think he had something to do with that."

The woman spun on me fast. I lifted my arms in case I had to defend myself.

She stuck her calloused finger in my face. "Rob did nothin' to dat man. He was nowhere near him. He quit on Thursday like I told him to. Darren had no honor."

So Rob quit the day before Darren's body was found. That brought me back to wondering how Darren was planning to serve barbecue without a cook? What was the BBQ Fixin' truck doing at that location?

I gulped and nodded. "That's good. Then he will be fine once he tells the police he has an alibi."

The woman put down her finger. Her hardened face softened. She said nothing else to me, but turned around. I let out a sigh of relief. Rob had someone in his corner. And somebody else had pegged Darren as a bad person. I just hoped Rob didn't get hurt in the process.

I looked past the sweetgrass basket booth where the woman had returned to the basket she'd been working on. To my surprise, I saw Chris coming toward me. He carried Tyric on his hip and Kisha skipped beside him. Bringing up the rear was Leesa, who looked as nauseous as I was feeling.

Chris stopped in front of me. "Everything okay, Ms. Eugeena?"

I yelped, "I don't know. Wilkes and a few officers just chased the poor man at his booth."

Chris raised his eyebrows at me. "That man, as you already know, needed to be brought in for questioning."

Leesa rolled her eyes. "No need to pretend, Mama."

I sighed. "I wasn't pretending. We came to enjoy the market today in case Wilkes asks."

Chris shook his head. "And you thought it was a good idea to have a conversation with Darren's cook? Let's go." He herded us away from the crowd, scolding. "Did you know he had a police record?"

Leesa and I exchanged looks.

I responded. "Well, that kind of information wasn't publicly available. And the man apparently has been allowed to set up a booth here." I held up the walking stick. "He must have redeemed himself by making products like this."

With his frustration clear in the set of his jaw, Chris said in a low voice. "You shouldn't be butting into police matters. You don't know what you're getting involved in."

Leesa huffed. "We didn't do anything wrong." Her face brightened, although her fiancé was obviously not happy with either of us. "At least this means Marcus is off the hook, right?"

Chris shifted Tyric in his arms, his expression grim. "Unfortunately, Marcus isn't in the clear. But he's not the focus anymore."

I wanted to ask more questions, to understand what was going on, but I held my tongue as I caught sight of Wilkes. The two deputies were moving through the crowd with Rob. Rob held his head low.

But did Rob do anything to Darren? Not according to his sister, who trailed behind talking to Wilkes.

MARINATED CONDITIONS

I was afraid Wilkes and Chris were going to keep grabbing the wrong person for Darren's murder. What were we all missing?

As soon as I walked through the door, I couldn't wait to tell Amos what happened at the farmers market. I found him sitting in his chair on his phone. And by the looks he was giving me, I already knew Chris was in his ear.

This was not how you made things good with your soon to be mother-in-law, Chris.

I headed past Amos to the stairs. For a change, Porgy followed behind me like he was my shadow. He either thought I had something for him or was ready to comfort me after Amos told me off. I'd stripped out of my clothes, freshened up, and pulled one of my favorite caftans over my head by the time I left the bathroom.

Amos was sitting on the bed waiting for me.

"How long have you been sitting there waiting to tell me what's on your mind?"

Amos shook his head. "You went there to talk to that man after we said it could be dangerous."

"First, before you go 'I told you so,' the man is harmless." I reached for the walking stick I bought for Aunt Esther. "He is also talented. His sister, the sweetgrass basket lady, had his back. She will tell Wilkes, if she bothers to interview and listen to her, that her brother quit before Darren was killed."

Amos opened his mouth, but I was tired and wanted to get my say. "And when I talked to Rob, he said he saw that Darren was no good. He wanted no part of that food truck, so why would he kill the man?"

I crossed my arms, waiting for the answer.

Amos looked at me and held up his hands. "Okay, it appears you gathered some good information while you were there, but..."

I sat on the bed and kept my mouth closed. Amos and his "but" statements were going to take the rest of my energy.

Amos continued. "Yes, he's been a good member of society running his own woodcarving business. But the man has a record of drug trafficking, Eugeena. He served his time and got out about four years ago."

I frowned. "I guess that's why he ran."

Amos raised his eyebrows. "He ran?"

"Yeah, he took one look at Wilkes and it was like he knew she was law enforcement. The man took off and left all his good work sitting at that booth. That made no sense, but I guess he was scared."

Amos clasped his hands together. "But you said he quit?"

"That's what I was told. You know, Rob seemed to be talking about Darren wanting to do something illegal. I wondered if Darren wanted to pull Rob back into dealing drugs."

Amos nodded. "That could absolutely be a possibility. Darren wanted easy money. Now nothing in his record came up, but that could mean he never got caught. And I know of cases where a food truck was the perfect venue for dealing drugs."

I wondered if Darren's death was a result of getting mixed up with someone not happy with his choices. I'd watched numerous television shows and knew there was always someone up higher with the real supplies and cash flow. Chris said Darren had been shot in the head. Cartel, maybe? I shuddered.

We sat for a few moments as theories marinated between us. That's when I remembered something more plausible. "You want to hear something strange that Rob mentioned to me?"

Amos looked at me.

"There's more to LaShonda and Darren's relationship than meets the eye. Did you know she gave him a large amount of cash? Rob saw it. She gave her ex-husband, the man who went off and had a baby with a younger woman, an envelope full of cash. Why would she do that?"

"That's a good question. Maybe she felt obligated?" Amos tilted his head. "Or she could have been threatened."

"I know she owns her own insurance company. Would she be bringing in big bucks?"

Amos nodded. "Depending on her clientele and the type of insurance she offers, she could. That is interesting. One thing that strikes me about Darren's death is the person had to know how to handle a gun and two, they had to be furious to shoot a man point blank. I don't know if we had a chance to talk, but I got a peek at the autopsy. Whoever shot Darren was facing him. They aimed the gun at his head."

My eyes widened. "They would have had to be a really good shot." I slapped my thigh. "Another reason they will not clear Marcus yet. I know Chris wants us to leave this alone, but we can't just sit back and do nothing. I wonder if LaShonda knows something that could clear Marcus's name."

Amos studied me for a long moment, his eyes searching mine. "How do you intend to find out this information?"

I shrugged. "I will probably have to have another conversation with her, but next week. Tomorrow is Sunday, and we're not doing any investigative work on the Lord's day."

He chuckled. "Sounds like a plan. But we need to think this through and make sure you have a proper plan. I don't want to be left in the dark while you and Leesa are out there playing detective."

I smiled, grateful for his support. "I'm telling you everything. Right now I need something to eat and an afternoon nap."

Amos patted my shoulder. "Sit tight, I will bring you a sandwich."

In all the excitement, I hadn't eaten since break-fast. I pulled the covers back and settled underneath. Though my body was ready to relax, my mind raced with questions.

Somebody really hated Darren to face him and shoot him point blank. Sometimes it wasn't the most obvious person.

Chapter 17

Sunday dinner today had more people than last Sunday, but there was still some tension. Cedric and Carmen both had the day off together for a change. After the meal, Cedric took charge of his niece and nephew outside, while Carmen and Leesa helped me clear off the table and clean up in the kitchen. Leesa had been quiet for most of dinner. I assumed because Chris was absent.

"Did Chris go to church today with Belinda?"

Chris's mother had been over a few times, but I could tell she wasn't comfortable outside her own home. Since the engagement, Belinda had been trying to appear like she would be a good mother-in-law. Chris was her only child and she'd been widowed over a decade. Occasionally, she liked to keep Chris to herself.

Leesa was drying the dishes after I rinsed them. "Yes, he attended church with her today."

"So is everything good after yesterday?" I'd called Leesa and even texted her to see how things went after the farmers market, but I hadn't heard from her until today.

Leesa placed the last plate in the cabinet before turning around. "He's not upset about yesterday anymore. They let Rob Wallace go. Like you said, his sister provided an alibi for him and he'd already quit working for Darren."

Carmen, my daughter-in-law, looked from me to Leesa as we talked. Both she and Cedric were out of the loop about Operation Food Truck Mystery. She questioned Leesa. "But you seem down about something."

I was thankful my daughter-in-law said it instead of me. Sometimes things came better from a peer than your mama.

Leesa grimaced. "I might as well show this to you before someone tells you about it."

Carmen and I exchanged a look after Leesa left the kitchen. She shrugged while my apprehension rose.

What is going on now?

Leesa came back to the kitchen with her phone. She sat at the table. I sat on the other side and waited as Leesa appeared to be pulling up a post on social media.

"Don't say anything yet? Just watch."

I adjusted my glasses on my nose so I could look down at the video. I pressed play. The video showed Sasha and Jada engaged in a heated argument at the crime scene. There was me on one side trying to pull Sasha back, and Leesa on the other side. The women's voices hurled insults at each other. Even though I was there, I didn't remember them being quite that vicious.

"Lord, Sasha was about to smack Jada if we hadn't pulled her back. Who took this video?" I knew people like to take videos with their phones, but I didn't particularly like that they'd captured this scene.

Leesa sighed. "I don't know who took the video, but the account is @Spill_The_Tea_Sis. It's a popular gossip account. Anyway, the account got back to Wilkes. Someone mysteriously sent this link to her. Chris was already on her nerves, but she told him last night, as of Monday, he's off the case."

Carmen sputtered. "What? For a social media post. You and Ms. Eugeena were trying to help."

Leesa blew out a breath. "That's not all. Y'all saw the video, but you didn't read the comments." She took her phone back and scrolled.

@JadaG_Slay: I don't know who posted this video, but I want the world to know that @SashaG_26 and her man are losers. A good man's life was taken because of them being jealous.

"What? Why is Jada trying to tell the world that Sasha and Marcus were jealous of Darren?" I was so confused.

"It gets worse, Mama. Hit the replies."

I squinted and hit the comments below @JadaG_Slay.

@SashaG_26: Don't be starting stuff on social media. You always been a liar.

@JadaG_Slay: I'm the liar. You know what y'all did. You and @LeesaPatt93 always acted like you were too good for people. That's why you both had them babies young.

I slapped the table with my hand. "Wait a minute now." This girl was throwing shade here on social media because Leesa and Sasha had their kids young.

Leesa placed her hand on mine. "Calm down, Mama. This is how she has always been. She gets things on people and then bullies them about it. But look what Sasha says."

@SashaG_26: At least I ain't I lied about the paternity of my baby.

@LeesaPatt93: Thank you @SashaG_26. This ain't high school @JadaG_Slay. My life is fine right now. Sounds to me like you need to get yours together.

"Oh, my Lord." I held my hands to my chest. My daughter and her friend were trading insults on social media.

"Wow," Carmen said. "Y'all went in on her. Look at the rest of these comments."

I held my hands against my face. "I can't believe Sasha put the question of her son's paternity out there in public like that."

Leesa's face was etched with worry. "But did you see what she wrote about Sasha and me, about having babies young? That was cruel."

"It was very cruel. And this is why Wilkes pulled Chris off the case?"

Leesa sighed, running a hand across her ponytail. "After seeing that, it was the last straw for her. She thought the whole thing had become too personal for him."

I raised an eyebrow. "How did Chris take it?"

Leesa shrugged, a hint of disappointment in her voice. "He seemed relieved, to be honest. But he's also disappointed in me for getting so involved. I told him I had to defend myself. He thinks we need distance, that we shouldn't use Sasha and Marcus as our caterers anymore. But with two months to go, it would be virtually impossible to secure another caterer."

I felt a pang of sympathy for my daughter, knowing how much this case had been impacting her relationship with Chris.

"Leesa," I said gently, "if this case isn't solved as we get closer to your wedding, what will you do?"

Leesa's eyes filled with tears, and she shook her head. "I don't know, Mama," she whispered. "I want to be there for Sasha and Marcus, but I also don't want this to ruin my wedding day."

Carmen, who had been listening quietly, reached out and squeezed Leesa's hand. "You shouldn't have to choose between your friends and your happiness."

There were so many things about this case that touched my family way too close.

I still intended to get some answers, but like Amos warned, I needed to stay under the radar.

Chapter 18

I walked into Palmetto Insurance Solutions offices around eleven o'clock in the morning. I wasn't sure if I could just show up, so I'd made an appointment this morning. Amos wanted to go with me, but I talked him out of it. I felt like if I went by myself, I could establish the same rapport that I had last week with LaShonda.

I hoped to talk to her about her annuity services. My oldest son was an attorney and talked about how he'd set up annuities for him and his wife. It was hard to listen to your children talk about retirement, but I was glad they were thinking ahead. Between our pensions and social security, Amos and I lived pretty comfortably and not above our means. We both talked about leaving something for our children after we were gone, so the annuities conversation sounded like a good segue into what I really wanted to ask.

I could tell from LaShonda's home that she must have done well for herself. Teaching wasn't for her, but the Lord led her to something she'd become good at and excelled. The receptionist greeted me with a warm smile. She appeared to be LaShonda's age, early forties. The woman wore a smart salt and pepper bob with thick black glasses.

"Good morning! How can I help you?"

"Good morning," I said. "I made an appointment this morning with Ms. Clark."

The receptionist nodded. "It's Mrs. Patterson-Jones, correct?"

"Yes, that would be me."

The woman whose nameplate on her desk read 'Jackie' said, "Have a seat and she will be right with you. She has another client in her office right now."

I walked over to the cozy waiting room area that had a couch and two plush chairs. I chose the chair by the window to sit in and grabbed a *Southern Living* magazine. These magazines were beautiful to look at, but too high fashioned for me, so I put it back.

Instead, I peered around at the walls of LaShonda's insurance office and became fascinated by the photographs. They looked like someone had taken photos of Sugar Creek and the surrounding areas of Charleston. They were quite nice, and I wondered who the artist could be.

It was probably time for me to go to the eye doctor again. No amount of squinting through my bifocals helped me read the artist's scrawl in the right-hand corner of the matte. The first letter looked like an "A" but I could not interpret the scrawl. I'd seen so much chicken scratch over the years from my students, I started insisting in my later years that they print their names only.

Probably part of the reason I wore bifocals now.

I heard loud voices and turned around from my examination of the photos to see where the commotion had come from. LaShonda's door had been flung open.

A young woman walked out. As she marched toward me, she glanced my way and paused, but then she moved forward, shoving open the glass door of the office as if she was in a hurry.

It was Jada. She'd worn a turban on her head and also glasses.

Why would she come to visit Darren's ex-wife?

Jackie said, "Mrs. Patterson-Jones, you can come back now."

I stepped inside LaShonda's office. For a few minutes, she stared at me as though she didn't recognize me. Then she plastered a smile on her face.

"Mrs. Patterson," she said, rising to her feet. "Have a seat. What brings you here today?"

"You can call me Eugeena." I took a seat across from her, my mind racing with questions I wanted to ask. Seeing Jada come out of her office took my breath away. Not sure where to start, I eased my way into my intended conversation. "Those photos in your waiting room are beautiful. Is that a local artist?"

LaShonda beamed. "That is a local artist and you know him."

"I do?"

"That's Ace's work. He had a bad few years once in he started attending high school, but his junior year he took a photography class and that really got him back to himself." LaShonda's smile dimmed. "He didn't handle college too well, but he always had his photography to help him. He helps the company by taking photos of properties we insure or assess."

Ace. That made sense, thinking of the signature in the corner again.

"That's great. College isn't for everyone and doesn't have to be." I glanced around the office. "You must be doing well for yourself."

LaShonda smiled proudly. "I've been focusing on commercial property insurance for a little over ten years now. It was a bit of a learning curve at first, but I've built a strong client base and a great team. I feel blessed to help local businesses protect their assets."

"Oh, then I'm not sure if you can help me. I've been retired for a while now. My oldest son mentioned annuities to me over the holidays. To be honest, it was a confusing conversation, but I thought it wouldn't hurt to find out more. Do you do that too?"

LaShonda smiled warmly, leaning forward in her chair. "Annuities can be a great way to ensure a stable income in retirement and leave a legacy for your children. I'm happy to explain how they work and answer questions you may have."

I nodded, feeling more at ease. "That would be wonderful. My son tried to explain it, but I'm afraid it went right over my head."

LaShonda chuckled. "Don't worry, that's a common reaction. Annuities can seem complex at first, but they're quite simple once you break them down. Essentially, an annuity is an insurance product that provides a guaranteed stream of income in retirement. You invest a lump sum or make a series of payments, and the insurance company pays you back."

"I see," I said, trying to wrap my head around the concept. "And how does that help with leaving something for my children?"

"Well, depending on the type of annuity you choose, you can set it up so that if you pass away, the remaining payments will go to your beneficiaries — in this case, your children. It's a way to ensure they receive a steady income even after you're gone."

I nodded, impressed. The woman knew her stuff. I still didn't understand why LaShonda would give her ex-husband money. She seemed like a sensible woman. But that question would come soon enough.

"And you offer these services? Property insurance? Annuities?"

She paused for a moment. "As for annuities, that's a more recent addition to our services. About four years ago, I partnered with Ray, who has his own insurance business. You met him last week at my house."

This was intriguing. "Yes, I remember him. Handsome man."

"He is." LaShonda blushed. "Ray specializes in life and health insurance, including annuities. We work together to offer our clients a more comprehensive range of products."

"How does the partnership work?"

"Well, Ray and I remain independent business owners, but we collaborate closely. When one of my commercial clients asks about annuities or other life insurance products, I refer them to Ray. And when his clients need property insurance for their businesses, he sends them my way. It's a win-win situation for everyone involved."

"That sounds like a smart arrangement," I said. "So if I'm interested in annuities, you would send me to him?"

"Yes, we share office space. Jackie can set you up an appointment for later today. He could explain this all better than me." LaShonda reached for her phone.

I held up my hand to stop her. "Not yet, give me just another minute. I'm curious to know if your commercial property insurance business insures restaurants, and would that include food trucks too?"

LaShonda's expression shifted. Her brow furrowed slightly as she registered the change in my line of questioning. She leaned back in her chair, studying me for a moment before responding.

"Yes, our commercial property insurance can cover restaurants, including food trucks." Her tone was measured. "We work with business owners to create policies that protect their specific assets, whether that's a brick-and-mortar location or a mobile operation." She paused then added, "But I have a feeling that's not really what you're asking about, is it?"

I met LaShonda's gaze, sensing the tension in the room. "I apologize if I'm overstepping, but I recently learned that you invested in your ex-husband's food truck business. I was wondering if that's something you typically do for clients."

LaShonda's jaw tightened, and I could see a flash of anger in her eyes.

For a brief second, I wondered if there was more to this former teacher than I knew. Maybe she was invested in Darren's business for a different reason. It took money to run your own insurance company.

Chapter 19

I watched LaShonda's shoulders droop. Any spark of a fight faded from her eyes. She spoke slowly, as if weighing each word with caution. "I understand you may be curious, given the recent tragedy with Darren's death. And you and your family sound close to the Greenes. I'm sorry about Marcus being under police scrutiny."

She'd picked up a fancy ballpoint pen from her desk. And I'm not even sure if she realized it, but the entire time she talked, she rolled it back and forth in her palms. It was a little distracting, so I tried hard to focus on her face.

LaShonda continued talking, not even looking at me. Her eyes were focused over my head. "But I can assure you that my investment in his business was a personal matter, not a professional one. It has no bearing on the services I provide to my clients."

"Of course not. I wasn't insinuating that at all, LaShonda," I said softly. "I'm wondering why Darren set out to alienate Marcus and Sasha. They said he wasn't really interested in the business. Why start the food truck back up? You said yourself he should have let it go. Luke Greene started that business."

LaShonda sighed as she leaned back in her chair. She appeared tired, like the last few minutes weighed heavily on her. "You know, I had no intentions of giving Darren money for anything. I did it for Ace. Most of the things I do are for my son."

I nodded. "I can understand that. If you don't mind me asking, how did you meet Darren? The more I learn about him... he seems like an interesting character."

LaShonda scoffed. "That's a nice way of putting it." She crossed her arms and moved her head from side to side as if preparing herself to tell me the story. I imagined the tension I'd brought in with me didn't help.

She smiled, her voice sounding dreamy. "My first love was Ray. He'd been my everything since I was thirteen years old. He's always been a bit of hottie!" LaShonda threw her head back and laughed. "My mother and her sisters used to tell me, 'you sure know how to pick 'em.'"

I could almost hear Annie Mae and Willie Mae, in my ear, saying that to their niece.

"I was hurt when Ray went into the Army," she admitted. "But he didn't have a way to go to college like I did. The military was the best route for him. I met Darren while I still was a struggling college student. I'd grown lonely and those letters from Ray were so few and far between. I felt like I wasn't really enjoying my college years hanging on to this long distance relationship. Darren was charming, good-looking, and had a great sense of humor. He'd been hanging around, partying, and not the least bit interested in getting an education. But I fell for him. Then, I got pregnant with Ace, and my focus shifted to my son." LaShonda leaned forward, her eyes brightening again. "Ace was so smart and precocious. Eugeena, you remember him from your classes?"

"I do. Believe me, I've had a lot of students over the years, but he stands out," I smiled as I recalled the bright young boy who had shown such promise. "He was something else. Could quote historical facts like no other student I've ever had. You mentioned that Ace works for you doing photography work. I know young people don't stay on one thing for long these days. Did he have any interest in helping with the food truck?"

LaShonda faltered a bit. "Oh, I don't know. Ace has always wanted to please his father and have a relationship with him. Ace and his father hadn't been talking to each other for several years. Darren mentioned it would be good for Ace to help with the food truck. I had been meaning to run it by him."

That didn't seem like what she'd said earlier.

Didn't she say she gave money to Darren for Ace? Maybe she wanted Ace to see his father doing something solid. I wondered what Darren's employment was prior to the food truck.

I thought back to the crime scene. Ace was there skulking around in the background. I wondered what would have caused Ace to not want anything to do with his father?

My heart raced at her words, and I knew I had to ask the question. "LaShonda," I said slowly, "with Luke's death, and then Darren's death, do you think the food truck could have been a front for something else?"

LaShonda's eyes met mine, a flicker of fear passed over her features. "I don't know. I hope not." Her voice faded as the realization of what I said seemed to hit her. "I wouldn't be surprised if Darren had gone beyond selling barbecue, but... Oh my God!" She pressed her hands against her lips. "I shouldn't have given him the money. What if he used it for something illegal? Is that what the police think got him killed?"

I held up my hand. "Wait! Let's not jump to any conclusions. I'm sorry, I didn't mean to make you panic."

The woman looked like she was going to be ill.

I leaned forward. "Are you sure you're okay?"

She clasped her hands over the desk. "Yes. It's just that Jada came in here."

I gripped the arms of the chair as I recalled the anger on Jada's face as she left the office a few moments ago. "Why would she come here? She was at the house last week too. I hope she's not stirring up trouble."

LaShonda sighed heavily, placing her head in her hands. She looked at me, her eyes brimming with tears. "Oh, Eugeena, it's a mess. Jada came here accusing me of taking Darren away from her son. That I could have helped instead of being spiteful toward her and her son."

I raised an eyebrow, intrigued. "What? I don't understand the point of the accusation."

First, Jada got into it with Marcus and Sasha. Then, she argued with Rob at the market. I could understand the need to know who was responsible for Darren's death, but she couldn't just go around accusing people.

LaShonda ran her hand under her eyes. "Apparently, Jada and Darren's ...son has a serious medical condition. Darren needed money for his treatment."

Okay, that I didn't see coming.

"Darren came to me for money a few days before his death." LaShonda admitted, her voice strained. "But he never mentioned the boy. He wanted me to give him the funds for the food truck. But Eugeena, he didn't just ask. He threatened me."

I leaned forward. "Threatened?"

She nodded her head, a pained expression on her face. "It doesn't matter now. The point is, I didn't know about their son's condition. Ace stayed in the hospital for the first three years of his life. Darren knew how our struggles were and that I knew about having to care for a sick child. I thought Darren was being his usual manipulative self. If I had known the real reason, I would have helped in a heartbeat. Even if I don't like Jada, I would have paid the hospital bills directly. The boy deserves to have a good life like Ace."

I sat back, processing this new information. "So, Jada blames you for Darren's death, but you gave him money."

LaShonda nodded, her eyes glistening with unshed tears. "She didn't know I'd given Darren money. He didn't tell her. She thinks he got mixed up in whatever led to his murder. And like you, she thought Darren was into something else. That he got the money illegally."

"Darren put you in a difficult position."

LaShonda had a faraway look in her eyes. In a low voice, she said, "He blackmailed me. Did he even use the money to help his son?"

I got stuck on the word LaShonda had used herself.

Blackmail gave her a motive to murder her ex-husband.

But what secret did Darren take to the grave about on his ex-wife?

A knock at her door broke the tension that had arisen between us.

LaShonda looked at her watch and stared at the door. "That's probably Ray. He's bringing me lunch today." She stood and shook her hair as if to rid herself of the tense moment. "Come in."

Ray swung open the office door, a charming smile on his face and a brown paper bag in his hand. The aromas hit my nose, reminding me how long ago breakfast had been. I eyed the bag, noticing it was from across the street. One of my favorites, the Sugar Creek Café.

"Hey there, beautiful," he greeted LaShonda, his voice warm and affectionate. "I brought your favorite—a turkey club sandwich from the café you love and an ice mocha."

LaShonda's face lit up. She accepted the bag and drink, her earlier tension seeming to melt away in Ray's presence. "You're too good to me, Ray. Do you remember Mrs. Patterson?"

Ray's eyes landed on me. "Well, hello there. Nice meeting you again. You were at the house with your daughter and LaShonda's aunts."

I stood up, extending my hand. "Yes, I gave Annie Mae and Willie Mae a ride over. You can call me Eugeena." I turned to LaShonda. "I'm Mrs. Patterson-Jones these days."

LaShonda smiled. "Oh, you married again. I remember your husband was a doctor."

"Yes, he passed away about seven years ago. I'm married to a retired cop now."

"Oh," LaShonda's smile faltered. "No wonder you have so many questions."

I winked. "We learn a lot from our spouses. Speaking of marriage, what about you two? I definitely know a couple in love when I see them."

Ray grinned. "You never know. It's been on my mind."

LaShonda blushed. "Oh, Ray."

As I observed their interaction, I couldn't help but notice the ease and familiarity between them. Ray seemed to have a calming effect on LaShonda, his mere presence bringing a sense of comfort and security.

"I hope I'm not interrupting anything important," Ray said, glancing between LaShonda and me.

LaShonda glanced at me with a tight smile as she waved off his concern. "Not at all. Eugeena and I were catching up. Oh, and Eugeena was curious to learn more about annuities. Maybe we can set up an appointment with you."

Ray nodded as his eyes zoned in on me more closely. This man had sales agent written all over his face. He straightened the knot in his tie, which was already fine. "I will be happy to sit down with you and explain your options."

There was a certain intensity in his gaze. I could see why LaShonda's knees probably had gone weak in his presence since she was a teen. Even with the gray around his temples, the man had a dashing way of making you feel you were the only person in the room that interested him.

I gulped. "That sounds like a plan. I will talk to my hubby and see if we can get something set up soon. I will leave you two. I think I'm going to visit Sugar Creek Café myself for some lunch."

LaShonda smiled. "Thank you for stopping by."

I was pretty sure LaShonda was thankful that I was leaving. Right after Jada, she had to deal with my uncomfortable questions about Darren's business and her providing funds. I ventured to say that LaShonda hadn't had a good morning.

I waved goodbye to the secretary with my mind focused on food.

Once my stomach was satisfied, I would be back on the case.

Chapter 20

I stepped inside Sugar Creek Café, and the aroma of freshly brewed coffee and baked goods enveloped me. I knew Amos was out on an investigation with Joe, so I had some time to spare before heading home.

I needed to think about my next move.

Before approaching the counter, I couldn't help but notice the café was not far from where the food trucks were parked last Friday. It had been over a week since Darren's murder, and the killer still hadn't been found. I couldn't say I had any ideas. But I was sure it wasn't Marcus. The idea that he would seek revenge for his brother after all this time still didn't sit well with me. Marcus struck me as a devoted husband, father and son. Why would he jeopardize that? And he and Sasha felt no animosity or competitiveness with Darren coming back on the scene with Fixin' BBQ. The couple was getting their own accolades for Smokin' Ward.

Rob Wallace had an alibi. Despite his past drug trafficking record, he'd bailed on Darren too. Which made me wonder if Darren didn't have a cook, what was he doing with the food truck?

Then there were the people who made up Darren's family, LaShonda, Jada and Ace. I wasn't sure about any of them, either. They all had reasons to be angry with Darren. And Palmetto Insurance Solutions wasn't far from where the food truck had been parked.

"Hey there, Eugeena!" Joss Miller, my neighbor who lived next door with her grandmother Louise and a friend of Leesa's, greeted me with a warm smile. Joss was one of the baristas at Sugar Creek Café.

"Hi, Joss. How's it going?" I replied, returning her smile.

"Oh, you know. Same old, same old. How's Leesa doing after that whole social media mess?" Joss's face was etched with concern.

I sighed recalling the drama that had unfolded online. I didn't understand social media at all. Often being online felt like being in a different world where strangers had opinions and the audacity to have a say about other people's lives.

"Leesa's hanging in there. She doesn't want to give up on Sasha and Marcus as the caterers for the wedding."

Joss nodded in understanding. "I can imagine. Their business is just getting started and Leesa and Sasha have been friends for a long time." Joss looked around at the other patrons in the café before lowering her voice. "To be honest, this whole food truck incident has put a damper on business in the area. There's already been too much going on the past few months."

I sighed again, I was doing a lot of that these days. "You're right." Unfortunately, a shop owner had been killed last fall. That incident seemed to have a ripple effect, and businesses were fighting to stay open in the community as a land development deal loomed in the city council.

Since Joss mentioned it, I asked. "Were you working in the café that day?"

Joss pointed a finger. "Leesa mentioned y'all had been investigating some things. I was wondering when you were going to ask."

I cracked a smile. "You know how I like to get to the bottom of things. I think you can relate."

Joss had her own podcast, the *Cold Justice Podcast*. She liked to concentrate on old cold cases.

"Yes, ma'am." Joss grinned. "What is it you want to know?"

"Do you remember anything strange that day? Maybe someone came into the café."

She shook her head. "I recall it was a busier day than usual, but the food trucks weren't in view of the café, so I can't say I noticed anything."

"Well, I thought I would ask. If you think of anything, let me know." I knew Joss had a keen eye. "I came in to grab some lunch and rest for a bit." After placing my order for a turkey sandwich, I made my way to a booth by the windows and pulled out my phone. While waiting for my food, I found myself watching the video of Sasha and Jada's heated argument. Again.

It was interesting to look at. There I was on one side of Sasha and Leesa on the other. I rarely saw photos of myself and certainly not videos. What bothered me about that day was not so much the argument, but why had Jada come? Did she stop by to say something to Darren? How did she know his truck was there?

I heard the chime above the Sugar Creek Café door as it swung open. I looked up and paused.

Ace.

Today, Ace wasn't wearing a hoodie, but a button-down shirt and jeans. A backpack was slung around his shoulder giving him a more professional, studious appearance. He must have been doing work for his mother. I watched him and Joss exchange a few words before he headed to the back of the café.

When Joss delivered my lunch, I asked, "Wasn't that Ace Clark?"

Joss glanced over her shoulder and nodded. "Yeah, that's him. You know him?"

"He's a former student. I was just over at his mother's place of business."

Joss glanced across the street. "That's right. He works over at the insurance company with his mom. He's a talented photographer. I asked him about putting some of his photos up in the café. Every few months, he switches them out. He's really good. You should check them out."

I nodded. "I will take a look." After taking my time finishing my lunch, I approached the back of the café and found Ace adjusting some of his photographs on the wall.

"Ace?"

Ace turned, recognition dawning on his face. "Oh, hey, Ms. Patterson. Wow, I haven't seen you in a years and now I've seen you last week and this week too."

"I was just talking to your mother, and she mentioned you were a photographer."

"It's mainly for insurance claims," he explained. "Most of the time, I use a drone."

"A drone. You mean one of those machines that flies around?"

Ace grinned. "Yep, I can fly it up pretty high with controls." He pointed to a photo on the wall. "See that right there? That's Sugar Creek at about 350 feet up."

"Wow, that's beautiful." I nodded, impressed by his skills. I looked over at him. "How are you holding up, Ace?"

The young man shifted uncomfortably. "I'm not sure. It's been a lot to process."

"Do you have any ideas about what might have happened? I met Rob at the farmers market. He didn't seem to have any ideas."

Ace hesitated before responding. "I never thought Rob did anything. Nothing makes sense. Dad said a lot of things he had no business, but I can't think of who he would make mad enough to kill him."

"Were you planning to work on the food truck, too?"

Ace stiffened. "No, not really. I have plenty to do with my photography." He held up his phone and started snapping pictures of his work.

I watched him, suddenly thinking about the video that was on social media. I wondered who captured the video in the crowd. Both Jada and Ace were there at the crime scene. Surely Wilkes had talked to all of Darren's family.

"You seem to get along well with Jada. How's she doing?"

Ace looked at me, surprise on his face.

I smiled. "You know I taught a lot of students."

Ace nodded. "I bet. Jada is missing my dad. I know people think she didn't have feelings for him because she was younger, but she did."

Ace had a faraway look in his eyes, as if he had some feelings himself.

I looked at Ace, recalling his gentleness with the often rude young woman. "That's good that she has a friend like you around during this time. You can be a comfort to each other."

Ace suddenly looked shy.

I had a feeling Ace's feelings were deeper for Jada than he'd like to admit. "You really do care about Jada, don't you?"

Ace visibly gulped. "We've been close for a long time."

I wondered how close. I decided to turn my questions in another direction. "Ray seems like a good guy. I met him again too. He seems to treat your mother well."

Ace's eyes flashed with anger. "Ray is the reason my parents weren't together. My mom knows this. She likes to think I don't know, but my parent's marriage was over long before Jada entered the picture."

I knew my eyebrows shot up. I don't know if I had that kind of face or demeanor, but people liked to spill their feelings out to me. As a teacher, I often served as a therapist and surrogate mother to many of my students. Most needed a listening ear.

"I'm so sorry. I know this must all be traumatic to you. I pray the police find out something quickly." I paused, weighing my next question carefully. "Since Jada was so close to your father, are you sure she doesn't know what could have happened? Maybe he got into it with someone and they threatened him."

He shook his head. "No. She was all hung up on Marcus, but I know that family. I told Jada she was wrong to accuse them."

"That's right, you were close to Luke."

Ace sighed. "Yeah, I hung out with him and Marcus. The whole family is cool. I think Jada needs to blame someone because she feels alone."

"Doesn't she have family to support her?"

Ace shook his head. "Not really. Her whole focus is Dougie. He's in and out of the hospital. I was with Jada at the hospital that night," he confessed.

I leaned forward, my brow furrowed with concern. "The night your dad died? What happened?"

Ace took a deep breath. "Dougie. He's only three years old. After he was born, they found out he had a congenital heart defect. He'd been struggling to catch his breath, so Jada called 911. She couldn't get my dad on the phone, so she called me. That wasn't unusual, so I thought nothing about it. My dad was good at not returning phone calls and texts. Jada got a hold of my dad's phone and I showed her how to set up location sharing."

"Thank goodness for technology. So you could see where your dad was?"

Ace twisted his face. "Yeah, it showed he was downtown. At first I thought he'd gone to see my mom. He would do that from time to time, even though she didn't like how he dropped in on her."

That was interesting. I wondered if Ace knew his mother gave his father money. Not only that, Darren had been blackmailing LaShonda.

I tuned back in to hear Ace say, "The worst part is my dad never updated his emergency contact information, so they called my mom even though they haven't been together in years. She found out about his death before we did." A bitter smile tugged at his lips. "Just another reminder of how much of a mess my dad left behind."

I frowned. "So you and Jada found out what happened by tracking your dad's location? I saw you both at the crime scene. That had to be a terrible shock."

Ace's eyes widened. "Oh yeah. That's right, you were there. Yes, Jada was furious. She wanted to tell him off for not being available again for Dougie. When we arrived, we saw all the cops and the crowd. I knew something had happened but... I never imagined not seeing my dad again."

"Do you think your dad took on the food truck business to help with the medical bills?"

Ace's shoulders slumped. "I think so. Jada and my dad were struggling to keep up with Dougie's medical bills. Even with insurance, the constant hospital stays and medications were a lot. I wish I could do more."

I focused on the wall of photos. "Do you do photography as a business? I'm sure people would pay good money."

Ace's face brightened. "I've been told that. Even my mom suggested it. I'm not sure how to start."

"You know, we may need a photographer for my daughter's wedding in June. I will reach out and ask her."

Ace showed the first genuine grin I'd seen since catching up with him. He reminded me of the young man who'd been eager to learn all those years ago in my class.

"That would be amazing. Thank you, Mrs. Patterson. It was good to see you again."

"You too. Take care, Ace." I watched the young man saunter toward the front of the café and leave. From the large window, I could see him cross the street and enter the Palmetto Insurance Solutions office building.

I was glad to see him again. Thinking about what he said, I wondered if Darren talked to his ex-wife that night. What would they have talked about?

What did Darren have in his pocket to hold over his ex-wife?

Chapter 21

By the time I arrived home, it was much later in the afternoon. I was in the kitchen trying to figure out what to make for dinner when my phone pinged and rang at the same time.

A phone call and a text. What's going on?

A quick glance at the text alerted me to Leesa's arrival with the kids.

Leesa: OTW

On the way. It took me a long time to figure out this strange language that consisted of acronyms for phrases that could have easily been written.

The call was from Amos. I knew that by the photo I'd snapped of him a few months ago. He was dressed in his usual attire for yardwork, which comprised of overalls and a baseball hat that curled up around his head.

I picked up on the third ring. "Hey, you heading home soon?"

Amos chuckled. "I don't get a hello anymore."

I laughed alongside him. "Not with these phones displaying who's calling."

"I'm near the Chicken Shack. You want me to bring you a meal?"

As much as I loved food and cooking it, there were some days when it was hard to come up with something for two people. I wasn't as adventurous in the kitchen as I was when I was younger, so I cooked the same meals all the time. "You read my mind. I sure couldn't figure out what to fix for supper. And maybe get the family meal. Leesa and her munchkins will be over soon."

At that moment, the doorbell rang. "Oh, they were closer than I thought."

Amos chuckled. "Tell them to hold tight. I will be there with some food soon."

A few minutes later, I heard the front door open. Kisha and Tyric raced into the kitchen to give me some hugs. As fast as they showed up, they raced back to the barking Porgy. The dog laid around all day like he was saving his energy for the children.

Leesa had her hands full with the kids's backpacks. She slid into a chair at the kitchen table, dropping the bags on the floor beside her.

I eyed her as I pulled a chair out from under the table. My day of investigating still had me tired. "You look like you had quite a day. How did everything go today?"

Leesa pulled out her phone, grinning like she'd won the lottery. "It was pretty busy, but I had some time to do some digging."

I raised an eyebrow. "Oh, what have you been investigating?"

Leesa pursed her lips. "I was curious if there was anything to the paternity of Jada's son."

I frowned. "But that could just be a rumor. And is the paternity of her child important to Operation Food Truck Mystery?"

Leesa bobbed her head. "I think so. Suppose the real father had something against Darren. Anyway, let me show you what I found. If anything, you may find it interesting."

I waited, anticipating what my daughter had been spending her time doing when she should have been working. I hope she got her tasks done for her job today. I was retired and had plenty of time to be in other people's business.

"Look, there are a lot of pictures of her and Ace together." Leesa began scrolling through Jada's Instagram profile. "I had to go back a few years on Jada's account. Interestingly enough, about three years ago, she was hanging out with Ace. Look at these photos."

I thought Ace seemed awfully protective of Jada. He supported her more than his dad. And Ace didn't seem to have the best father-son relationship with his dad either.

I leaned over to look at Leesa's phone. There were several photos of Ace with Jada. In one photo, he had his arm around her. "Oh! That one is interesting!" I pointed to a photo of Jada sitting in Ace's lap. I moved my chair closer. "How long ago was this? They look like a couple here."

Leesa looked up from her phone. "Right! That's why I wanted you to see. This looks like it would have been before Jada went for the dad. Ace and Jada never declared a relationship in any of the captions, but it's pretty obvious they were close."

"He definitely cares about her. But how and why would she go for Darren? Like you said before, he was old enough to be her father."

Leesa shrugged. "From what I remember, Jada always dated older guys. Her boyfriend at the prom had attended high school years ago, but dropped out."

I still couldn't see the appeal. That had to create a lot of tension between Ace and his dad. Could there have been anger and jealousy?

"I want you to see Jada's account in recent months." Leesa scrolled up past the squares of photos, most of them selfies. She stopped on photos of a baby.

I leaned in. "So this is Dougie. He's a cutie. Oh, goodness." I touched my chest as Leesa scrolled through photos of the baby in the hospital. As she continued to scroll, there were various photos of the child playing and happy. Other times he would be laying in a hospital bed. "That poor child, regardless of who the father is, we need to pray for him to get well."

Leesa sighed. "I do feel sorry for Jada. She's never been the nicest person, but it must be hard to have your child sick all the time. They have a funding site where folks can donate online. She's asking for thirty thousand dollars. That's a lot."

"Probably a lot of hospital bills. See how we can help."

While Leesa explored the funding site, something occurred to me. When I talked to LaShonda yesterday, she said she didn't know this child was sick. But the child was three years old and Jada had pictures splashed all over social media. Wouldn't Lashonda have known from Ace or Darren, even other people? Her twin aunts, Annie Mae and Willie Mae were big gossips. I wondered if the woman was telling me the truth and if not, why would she lie?

Leesa peered at me, studying my face. "What's wrong? You have that look on your face."

"What look?"

"The one where you don't like something. Your eyebrows almost come together, and your glasses are almost falling off your nose."

I grimaced and pushed my glasses toward my face. "I think maybe Darren's ex-wife had issues with him more so than Jada. I'm sorry, Leesa. I know you don't like her, but it's not looking like she shot the father of her child. She needed Darren to help her and Dougie. But LaShonda was giving money to Darren. She flat out said he was blackmailing her."

Leesa's eyes widened. "Blackmail? What did he have on her?"

I shook my head. "She wouldn't say, but it seemed like Darren knew something about her past that she didn't want revealed. Also, talking to Ace earlier, Darren's location showed he may have visited with LaShonda hours before he died."

Leesa started to nod her head. "I see where you're going with this. The food truck wasn't that far from her office."

"Right, Darren could have parked it there and went to see her." It made me wonder if LaShonda had more to do with Darren's death than we initially thought. "I sure would like to know what he had to blackmail her about."

A male voice rang out behind me. "Blackmail. What are you two up to now?"

Leesa and I spun around to find Amos in the doorway with Chicken Shack bags. I thought I heard the front door open, but we'd been so deep into our discussion. What I wasn't expecting was to find Chris standing next to Amos. Both men, the retired homicide detective and the younger homicide detective, were looking at us like we'd been caught doing something we shouldn't.

It was Chris who'd asked the question and seemed to be waiting for a response.

I broke the silence, choosing to not answer at the moment. "Let's get the kids some plates and we can discuss these matters while we eat."

That settled it. No one wanted to let those delicious smells coming from the bags linger in the air. We moved to the dining room table so we all had plenty of room to spread out and pass around the chicken bucket along with the side dishes.

Kisha and Tyric were settled at the kids table in the corner, both with kids meals consisting of chicken fingers and mac and cheese.

Chris waited until we all had dug into our plates. "What's this about blackmail?"

Leesa exchanged a glance with me before stating, "Chris, you're off the case."

He raised an eyebrow. "That doesn't mean I don't still have an interest. Especially when my fiancé and

TYORA MOODY

my future mother-in-law are still running their own investigation."

"I wouldn't say we're doing all that, but yes, I've had a busy day." I filled Amos and Chris in on my earlier visit to LaShonda's insurance company and then my conversation with Ace at the café.

"LaShonda admitted she gave Darren money. She said the way he did it felt like blackmail though she did volunteer that Darren may have been trying to raise money for Dougie's medical expenses. It appears the man wasn't such a bad guy after all. But then... somebody killed him."

Leesa piped in with how close Jada and Ace were years ago, and how they still seemed to be good friends. "All of these people close to Darren seemed to have more motive to kill him. I hope Wilkes has placed Marcus off her list."

Chris responded. "Marcus should be in the clear. There were a couple of phone calls that stood out on Darren's phone, mostly Jada."

"Make sense. They were trying to get Darren to come to the hospital that night after Dougie was rushed to the emergency room. Ace felt like his dad stopped in to see LaShonda that night. Did you get impressions? I'm sure you had to talk to her."

Chris frowned. "We did talk to LaShonda Clark. She said that he'd called her, but she'd already closed up for the day. She had an event to attend. We checked it out and she had witnesses that saw her. She was a guest speaker so she had pretty good visibility that night."

"Oh, so he went to see her, but never spoke to her." I sighed, setting down my fork.

Chris rubbed his chin thoughtfully. "There are quite a few people who had a reason to want Darren gone. But every one of our suspects have been able to provide solid alibis."

I was glad Chris felt freer to share information. The tension from the past few weeks seemed to have cleared. It was like a scene from *Law and Order*, except it was all of us tossing theories while we devoured chicken wings and biscuits.

My mind raced. "Is Wilkes still looking at the drug trafficking angle?"

Chris reached for a piece of chicken. "Wilkes is still exploring if Darren went an illegal route. Rob Wallace wasn't a lead since he's moved on past his drug trafficking conviction years ago."

I brought up another angle that had been bothering me. "What about Luke? His case is still open and there were some similarities right? Could he have been killed because of what he knew about Darren, or were the two of them into something together with the food truck?"

Amos commented. "Detective Eugeena, you don't miss much."

We all laughed, but I noticed Chris seemed to be contemplating what I asked.

He looked at me. "That's something we should look into. Both men were shot. I'd be interested to see the comparison on the ballistics."

My eyes widened. "You mean the same gun could have been used on both of them. The same person."

Chris claimed all these people had alibis.

What and who were we missing?

Chapter 22

It took some convincing, but I told Leesa we finally needed to face Jada. Their school history and social media bickering would not help us find out what the woman knew. We'd seen her all over the place accusing people. It was time for a face-to face.

We'd been following Jada's updates on Dougie's condition. The little boy had been back home for a few days. Each day, Jada showed pictures of Dougie. Sometimes she was in the picture. One day there was a picture of Ace holding Dougie. The only other person I saw in the photos was a woman who could have been a relative.

Leesa parked in front of the home that we assumed had been shared with Darren. Of all the people to have their address, it was Annie Mae. I didn't ask her how or why she had the address, but she offered it up when I mentioned wanting to send a donation.

We sat in the car looking at the small home in an older, more run down section of Sugar Creek. This house needed a coat of paint and appeared shabbier than the rest of the surrounding homes. I noticed it didn't have a garage. Darren must have stored the food truck in another location.

Leesa and I exchanged looks. She asked, "Are you sure this is the right place? It looks so unkempt. Did Darren even live here?"

"It does make you wonder. Annie Mae seemed sure this was the address. If they've been taking care of a sick child, sometimes things get neglected. If it's the wrong place, we will hightail it out of here."

"Okay," Leesa sighed. "I wish there was another way to do this. You know I don't like her."

"Put your feelings to the side for now. We're here to show support for her and Dougie. That's all that matters."

With Leesa carrying a basket filled with donations for Jada and her son, we approached the front door. I knocked on the door and we waited. I couldn't hear any activity, so I knocked again.

Leesa said, "We can leave the basket at the front door."

"We will not. Not in this neighborhood."

The front door opened with a jarring noise, like it had been stuck. A chain held the door in place, and when Jada looked out, her eyes narrowed in suspicion.

"Mrs. Patterson?" Her eyes switched to Leesa beside me. "Leesa, what are you doing here?" she asked.

I expected to hear anger or attitude in her voice, but all I heard was a bone weary, tired woman. A bit scared too.

I stepped forward. "We wanted to bring you some things for you and your son. We know how hard it must be and wanted to show our support."

Jada eyed us some more before removing the chain and opening the door. Suddenly shy, she said, "You can come in. Dougie is sleeping, so you have to be quiet."

We entered the small home, which was cozy and neat. While the outside needed some maintenance, the inside smelled like roses. Streaks up and down the carpet indicated recent vacuuming.

Leesa handed her the basket, "Jada, I know we haven't always seen eye to eye, but I want you to know that we're here for you."

Jada took it from Leesa's hands. "Thank you," she said. Her voice sounded timid.

Trying to break the ice between the two tense women, I said, "My family wanted to make a donation to Dougie's medical care, but I wanted to put it in your hands instead of doing it online. I understand those websites take out a lot of fees, so you don't get the full amount."

Jada's eyes widened in surprise, and I could see a flicker of gratitude in her expression. "That's... that's very kind of you, Mrs. Patterson. I don't know what to say."

I smiled, feeling a sense of relief that we had bridged the gap between us. "You don't have to say anything. We want to help in any way we can."

"Please have a seat. Would you like anything to drink? I only have bottled water and juice."

"Bottled water will be fine."

When Jada disappeared into the kitchen, Leesa made a strangled noise behind me. I shushed her and pointed to the couch. She rolled her eyes and sat on one end of the couch while I sat on the other.

Jada came out with two bottles of water, handing us one each. "Thank you for bringing these things. I haven't seen much of anybody except my sister and Ace. They both have to work. Even though I hear a lot of comments on social media, it's good to have people to talk to in person."

This child is alone!

No wonder she'd been frantically reaching out for help. I wondered if Jada worked, or did she depend on Darren. Ace seemed to be very supportive. The question of Dougie's paternity popped into my mind. Ace mentioned he'd been close to Jada a long time. I wasn't sure how or if I should ask questions.

Leesa shifted uncomfortably on the couch. "How is Dougie doing, Jada? Is there anything else we can do to help?"

Jada's shoulders slumped, and I could see the exhaustion and worry etched on her face. "He's stable for now, but the doctors say he'll need more treatments in the future. I don't know how I'm going to afford it all. I don't know what Darren got into, but I really needed his support."

"Jada, do you have any idea who might have done this to Darren?" The girl had accused so many people over the past few weeks. I wondered if she knew or was she just looking for someone to blame.

Did any of the money Darren got from LaShonda actually make it to Dougie's care? Rob had mentioned it was a wad of cash in an envelope.

"No, I don't have any idea. But I saw Darren with a lot of cash. I asked him about it, but he wouldn't tell me where it came from. He paid off about half of what we owed. But then Dougie had to go to the ER the other night. I don't know what that bill will be yet."

Before I could stop myself, I blurted. "It's my understanding that Darren asked LaShonda for money before he died."

Jada's eyes widened in shock. "What? No, she wouldn't have given him money." Anger flashed in her eyes. "She thinks I'm the one who ruined her marriage. I doubt she cares anything about Dougie or me. I don't know where you heard that rumor, but LaShonda wouldn't give Darren a penny."

Leesa leaned forward. "So why were you at her office? My mom saw you. Are you sure you don't know anything about Darren blackmailing LaShonda or the secret she was hiding?"

I winced. Maybe we shouldn't have mentioned that. Now I was feeling uncomfortable.

Jada shook her head. "Blackmail? Secret? No, I know nothing about that. Darren mentioned nothing like that to me."

Small cries rang out from a room off from where we sat. "That's Dougie. Let me go get him."

When Jada left the living room, I sighed, realizing we may have overstepped and would not learn much from Jada. She'd been kept in the dark about Darren's actions. Maybe he didn't want her to know he went to his ex-wife for money. The same way he didn't want LaShonda to know he needed money for the baby he had with another woman. Seemed a complicated way to operate.

Jada came out of the room with Dougie in her arms. The toddler appeared smaller than an average three-year-old would be, but just as cute. His wide eyes soaked up us new people.

"Say hello," Jada urged the little one.

He offered a shy grin and a small wave.

Leesa and I both went over to coo at the young boy. He laughed like a happy boy. It warmed my heart to see him feeling better. So full of life as he should be instead of being hooked to wires on a hospital bed.

I reached out and placed a comforting hand on Jada's arm. "We're here for you, Jada. Whatever you need, please let us know."

Jada nodded, and I could see a glimmer of tears in her eyes. "Thank you. I appreciate you both coming here and bringing these things for us. It means a lot."

After Leesa and I climbed back in the car, Leesa said, "Well, that went better than I expected. She seems like a different person. I almost feel like there are two different Jadas."

"Sometimes people act one way, the way they think people expect them to act. This Jada is a concerned mother who's worried about what's going to happen to her and her child. We'll pray for them and keep up with her online updates."

Before Leesa started the car, she turned to me. "Is it bad that I'm still wondering if Dougie was Darren's son? With that boy in the hospital all the time, it seemed like that would have come up."

I raised an eyebrow. "If we're talking father and son, it depends on if they share the same blood type."

I still was curious myself. So far we'd only found signs of a possible romance with Ace prior to Jada hooking up with Darren. But I wasn't convinced the paternity angle had anything to do with Darren's death.

What I did feel good about was that neither Jada nor Ace were on my list of suspects. But I feel like the dynamics between LaShonda and her ex-husband needed further investigation.

Chapter 23

Leesa felt better after stopping by Jada's. She told me Jada sent her a thank you via DM. I didn't understand all the ways young people liked to communicate, but I was happy the two women could see eye to eye. They were both moms and those messy riffs from high school were in the past.

I anxiously waited for Detective Wilkes to do her magic and solve this case. Chris told us they were still waiting on the ballistics report. One thing I'd learned from Amos and Chris, real police work was not like television. It took a long time. With no news, Operation Food Truck Mystery was on hold for us amateurs.

So Leesa and I went back to wedding planning. I didn't realize that Leesa's photographer had canceled. With yet one more thing that could go wrong, Leesa reached out to Ace. He gladly accepted the opportunity. I had a feeling the young man was seeking ways to do his own thing, but needed more direction.

It had been two weeks since Darren's murder, and we arrived at Marcus and Sasha's home to discuss the catering for Leesa's wedding. As Leesa pulled into their driveway, I couldn't help but feel a mix of apprehension, but I wasn't sure why. Maybe because we parked behind the Smokin' Ward food truck, and a man's body had been found shot inside a similar truck.

I was suddenly curious about the inside of the food truck. The most I saw was Darren's body hanging out the back. But my brain wasn't focused on the crime scene, so I hadn't given it much thought. And, the man's feet were the first thing I saw. Either he was heading out of the food truck or maybe somebody knocked on the back of the door. Either way, he opened it, and probably briefly saw his shooter.

After we climbed out of Leesa's minivan, Marcus stepped out the back of their food truck, his face etched with a weariness that hadn't been there before. "Hey, Ms. Eugeena. Leesa. Sasha's finishing up in the kitchen."

"Leesa, you go on ahead and talk to Sasha. Marcus, would you mind giving me a tour? I've never seen the inside of a food truck."

Leesa turned to look at me. "Hey, I want to see too."

Marcus grinned. I could sense a mix of pride and nostalgia emanating from him. "Sure, I would be happy to. I just started cooking. We have an event on Friday and Saturday, so we have a busy weekend ahead. You may have noticed this is more of a trailer."

"Yes, I noticed you haul this around with your truck and that it's a lot longer than the Fixin' BBQ food truck. Looks like this is more customized."

Marcus nodded. "That's right. This is what my brother really wanted. I had all his drawings in a notebook he left. Let's start around the back of the trailer where the porch is located."

As a customer, I headed straight for the concession window to place an order. I was intrigued with seeing how this all worked behind the scenes.

"Welcome to the Smokin' Ward," Marcus announced, opening the half-door and gesturing for us to step inside. "This is where the magic happens."

As we entered the truck's porch, the mouthwatering aroma of slow-cooked pork barbecue immediately struck me. Marcus pointed to a large stainless steel smoker. "This is where we slow-smoke our pork for hours, infusing it with that signature Smokin' Ward flavor. We use a special blend of hickory and apple wood to give it a subtle sweetness and a nice, smoky depth."

"It smells so good!" Leesa commented.

We followed Marcus from the porch inside the trailer. At a glance, I could tell the compact interior was efficiently organized resembling a small industrial kitchen. As a fan of kitchens, this was a marvel! A tiny little restaurant on wheels.

I watched as Marcus pointed to a large prep table, its surface covered in cutting boards and various kitchen tools. "This is where we trim and season the meat before it goes into the smoker. We have our own secret blend of spices that started with our father. Luke developed the spices over the years."

I nodded, impressed by the level of care and attention that went into their cooking process. "It smells incredible in here," I remarked, inhaling deeply.

Marcus grinned, his eyes lighting up. "Once the pork is smoked to perfection, we shred it by hand. We like people to have options, so we pack up vinegar based sauce." He pointed to a stack of tiny containers on the counter. "And tomato based sauce."

I watched as Leesa peered into a large pot simmering on the stove. "Is this the tomato based sauce?" she asked.

"Yep," Marcus confirmed. "We make it in small batches to ensure the flavors are always balanced and fresh."

As we moved toward the back of the trailer, Marcus showed us the storage area, where they kept their supplies and ingredients. "Organization is key in a small space like this," he explained. "We have to make sure everything is easily accessible and that we don't run out of anything during a busy service."

Realizing how much work and dedication went into running a successful food truck, I asked almost reverently. "You and Sasha really put your hearts into this, didn't you?"

Marcus nodded, a wistful expression crossing his face. "We did. This truck was our dream, our way of sharing our love of barbecue with the world." He pointed to a framed image on the wall above the cutting board area. I hadn't noticed the photo of a man who had lighter skin and resembled Marcus.

"Is this Luke?" I asked.

Marcus stared at the portrait for a few seconds before answering. "Yes. Losing Luke was a huge blow, but I know he'd want me to keep our family legacy alive."

I studied the photo of Luke Greene some more. Something about his face and his build nagged me. "Looks like you are doing that. I'm so sorry that all this business with Darren has been a distraction and hinderance to you and your family."

As we stepped back out into the sunlight, Leesa said, "Thanks for the tour, Marcus. I'm going to go inside and talk to Sasha about the catering. I know she's wondering what happened to us." Leesa glanced at me, but I gave her a nod. She seemed to get that I wanted to stay and talk to Marcus a bit longer.

Once Leesa rounded the corner, I looked over at Marcus. He stared back at me, a curious look in his eyes. "I'm sure Luke would be proud of what you've accomplished."

Marcus swallowed and looked away. When he turned back toward me his eyes glistened with unshed tears. "Thanks, Ms. Eugeena. That means a lot."

"Marcus, I know I asked you before and I hope you've had some time to think. Did you ever suspect that Darren might have been involved in anything illegal? Something that could have gotten Luke killed?"

Marcus's head snapped up, his eyes widening. "Darren hung around shady people, people who served in jail or had bad habits. But I feel like Luke would have never kept Darren on as a partner if he knew the man had taken on criminal activities."

I nodded, but pressed on. "I know your brother was a good man, Marcus. You said you wondered why Luke was friends with Darren. Did Luke believe in loyalty? Sometimes, people can hide things, even from those closest to them."

Marcus shook his head, his expression pained. "Luke was loyal to a fault. But he was a God-fearing man. I can't believe that he would turn a blind eye, Ms. Eugeena. Luke trusted Darren like a brother. I'm not saying that wasn't a mistake on my brother's part. He certainly could have missed something."

I hesitated, then asked the question that had been nagging me since I glimpsed the photo of Luke. "Marcus, I hate to even suggest this, but... is it possible Luke's death was a case of mistaken identity?"

Marcus froze, his face going slack. "What do you mean?"

I took a deep breath, choosing my words carefully. "Well, from what I've heard, Darren had a way of rubbing people the wrong way. It's possible someone had a grudge against him. And from the photo I just saw, I'm wondering if Luke was similar in build and height to Darren? They also seemed to have similar complexions."

Marcus's eyes widened, realization dawning. "You think someone might have shot Luke thinking he was Darren?"

I nodded, my heart heavy. "It's a possibility we can't ignore. And with the food truck back out in the open, someone might have finished what they started with Darren."

Marcus slumped against the trailer. "I always thought Darren had something to do with my brother's death. The way he hid the Fixin' BBQ food truck away all that time. It never made sense."

"I know it's a lot to take in, Marcus. But we're going to sort this out. We won't let Luke's death be in vain. I do have one more question, and I'm sure I've probably asked this before too. Is there anyone your brother might have been aware of that had issues with Darren? Maybe Luke saw an argument and mentioned it to you. If they were close friends, Luke had to have seen or known who Darren's enemies were, don't you think?"

Marcus rubbed his beard. I could tell he was taking his time thinking. Then he said, "You know the old detective on the case asked that same question. I told him the only person who agitated Darren was the guy that LaShonda ended up being with after their divorce."

I raised my eyebrow. "Ray Johnson."

Marcus nodded. "Darren hated him. Luke told me Darren talked trash about that man all the time. He thought LaShonda was cheating on him with Ray, but she kept telling him he was wrong. Luke told me how weird it was... Darren was accusing LaShonda of cheating, but he was cheating himself. He always had some young chick on the side."

I asked, "Was Jada in the picture back then? This is all about three, almost four years ago, right? Jada and Darren's son is about three years old."

Marcus shrugged. "Yeah, I guess, But I remember Jada was mostly with Ace. I'm not quite sure what the story is with her and Darren. Darren cheated a lot from what Luke said. But that sounds about right. LaShonda and Darren's divorce was final before Luke died. Darren stayed with Luke for a while until he got his own place. That's when my brother learned how much Darren resented Ray. Darren told my brother that Ray had always been waiting to swoop in."

Interesting.

Ray had been like a knight in shining armor for LaShonda. Thoughtful and considerate, but I wondered. Was there resentfulness and hate on Ray's part also? Sure, he finally got the girl in the end, but what was Ray thinking about after his girl had been stolen all those years ago?

"Thanks for talking to me, Marcus. I have a phone call to make."

I walked toward the house and pulled out my phone. Within a few seconds, Amos answered.

"Hey, Eugeena, what's up?"

"Did you say that you knew the detective that used to be on Luke Green's case?"

Amos cleared his throat. "Yes, I know him. Something come up?"

"Let's say I would love to know more about Ray Johnson."

Chapter 24

As Amos and I settled into our nightly routine, my mind kept wandering back to the tangled web of relationships surrounding Darren's murder. Something unraveled as far back as three years ago. Even before Luke was killed, Darren cheated and got a young woman pregnant. An already splintered marriage finally broke down and collapsed. And LaShonda went back to a long lost love.

The one person who seemed affected the most was the son, Ace. As splits with parents often did, they left a child lost.

But really, what was on my mind was the secrets LaShonda had that her ex-husband knew. How critical were those secrets to his death? And did they have anything to do with Luke's death two years ago? Could it be possible that LaShonda knew something about Luke's death and never said anything? That one seemed unlikely, but once my mind started going, I couldn't stop.

"You've been quiet." Amos said. "Seems like the conversation you and Leesa had with Jada has you thinking a lot."

"It made me more curious about the dynamics between LaShonda, Darren, and Ray. Darren was bold enough to go to LaShonda."

Amos fluffed his pillow. "They were married for years and had a son together. And as you found out, Darren knew her secrets, whatever those might be."

"Exactly! Those secrets have to be the key to something. I know you did background checks on everyone. What did you find out about Ray Johnson?"

Amos laid his head on the pillow, his brow furrowed. "Woman, we're supposed to be going to bed. I believe you are worse than I was about letting go of a case."

I laughed. "I want to know so I can clear my head."

He chuckled. "Right. Okay, let me see what I can recall. I'm in the bed now, woman." He pointed at me like he was scolding me. But I knew Amos took me seriously when I had my theories. I'd been right before.

And sometimes wrong.

Amos rubbed his head as if he could see the files downstairs in his office. "Ray had a long and interesting military career. He retired when he was thirty-nine and officially started in the insurance business. I think what interested me most was how he became partners with LaShonda four years ago."

I frowned. "Did you find that out after I told you about him being with LaShonda?"

"Yeah, but that's not the part that piqued my interest. You know to own an independent insurance company you have to raise a lot of capital. And there are federal regulations that monitor and protect consumers from fraud. Ray must have saved up money."

"Would he have earned that in the military?"

Amos shook his head. "Not that kind of money. Maybe he was good at investing his money. Or he had good investors to help start his business."

I sat down on the edge of the bed, my thoughts swirling. "Ray seemed nice, but the last time I saw him, underneath, he reminded me of that car salesman who trailed after you at the dealership. He would have tried to sell me annuities that very minute."

Amos chuckled. "That's how they make their living. They gotta sell you on their product and services."

I climbed into bed and got under the covers. "Ace dislikes him. He made it clear that he believes Ray was the reason his parents weren't together. When I talked to Marcus, it sounded like Darren had suspicions about a relationship between his then wife and her first love."

Amos fidgeted under the covers, trying to find his sweet spot on the mattress. "Maybe the marriage fell apart when LaShonda formed this business partnership with Ray. But there could have been some romantic connection, too." He laid still and then looked over at me, a deep crevice in his forehead. "How are you trying to connect this back to Darren's murder?"

"I don't know. I could be as bad as Leesa. Leesa wanted to connect Jada to this whole thing. I believe Jada needed Darren's support to keep her son well and help with mounting medical expenses. And even though LaShonda is head over heels for Ray, I can't help but wonder if he's too good to be true."

Amos raised an eyebrow. "What do you mean?"

I sighed, trying to put my concerns into words. "I mean, how did Ray really feel about Darren? They had history, with LaShonda caught in the middle. And from what I've seen, Ray doesn't seem to like Jada either. He's super protective of LaShonda."

Amos considered my words. "Let me get this straight. After talking to Marcus and seeing Luke's photo, you're going on this mistaken identity theory. Right?"

"Yes, but it would have to be someone more out to get Darren, and Luke was in the way. Who was Darren's number one enemy at the time?"

Amos nodded. "I see where you're going. I'm not wrapping my head around why. Don't get me wrong. Ray has an exemplary firearms record. But in the end, he got the woman. Darren didn't seem like much of a threat to Ray to take drastic measures."

I felt a chill run down my spine at the thought. "But what if Ray knew about the blackmail? Remember, he's protective of LaShonda."

Amos reached for my hand, giving it a reassuring squeeze. "We can't jump to conclusions. We don't even know what LaShonda supposedly did for Darren to blackmail her. You said yourself that LaShonda didn't seem to tell the truth. She obviously still had feelings for Darren and wasn't proud of that. Thus, this exaggerated tale of blackmail."

I sighed. "I guess you're right. She did host the celebration of life gathering at her house for Darren. That always felt odd to me."

"Sounds like the woman still loved her ex-husband." Amos reached for the covers and scooted further down under them. "I'm still thinking Darren got caught up in something illegal."

I knew Amos could be right, but wouldn't Wilkes have discovered a connection by now? I couldn't shake the feeling that I was on the verge of uncovering something significant. A lightbulb went off in my head. I already knew Amos wouldn't like it, but he wouldn't want me to do this alone.

"Amos, we should make that appointment."

Amos mumbled, his face in the pillow. "What are you talking about now, Eugeena?"

"We should see Ray Johnson. Make the appointment to discuss annuities. We have been meaning to do that anyway."

With a deep sigh, Amos rolled over and eyed me for several moments. "You're not going to let this go, are you?"

"Don't you want to know how the man felt about Darren? You're the one with experience. You can probably tell a lot more about him by talking to him. You haven't even met him yet."

He rubbed his head. "What can it hurt? Set up the appointment and we will meet this Ray guy together."

I leaned over and kissed him. "Thank you, partner."

I felt it in my spirit. I was onto something.

Chapter 25

Amos and I walked into the Palmetto Insurance Solutions office. I had scheduled an appointment to discuss annuities first thing this morning. The friendly receptionist, Jackie, sat at the desk and greeted us.

"Hello, so good to see you again, Mrs. Patterson-Jones." She smiled at me and then turned to Amos. "You must be Mr. Jones."

Amos stepped up beside me. "Good afternoon." Dressed in a blue polo shirt and khaki slacks, he'd cleaned up from doing his weekly yard work.

"Welcome to you both. Mr. Johnson will be with you in a few minutes."

We headed over to the waiting room where I'd sat earlier this week on Monday. As we sat down, the door to LaShonda's office opened. She appeared to be talking on the phone. Whoever was on the phone had the woman upset. "Just come to me and let's talk. I don't know where you are getting this information from."

LaShonda glanced up realizing someone was in the waiting room. She caught my eye. I waved at her, but she didn't wave back. In fact, she didn't look too pleased to see me at all.

"Eugeena?" She said.

"Hello, LaShonda. I told you I would come back with my hubby to talk to Ray about annuities."

"Oh," She looked over at a closed door and then back at us. With some effort, she put a smile on her face. "That's wonderful. I hope Ray can help you." She walked over. "I haven't met your husband."

Amos stood. "Amos Jones. Heard a lot about you."

"Oh," LaShonda said again, only this time her voice faltered.

"Your business and the services you offer," Amos explained.

"Good. I'm glad you've heard good things." LaShonda's attention seemed to be elsewhere. She peered out the windows of the office as if she was expecting someone. I wondered who she had been talking to on the phone.

I didn't have much time to think about it. The office door to our left opened and out stepped Ray Johnson. It must have been the military man in him, despite it being almost three o'clock in the afternoon, he appeared sharply dressed as if it was early morning. He reached for his tie to make sure it was still knotted perfectly.

Ray flashed us a bright, white smile. "Hey, folks, you came to see me."

We both stood. "Yes," I said. "We're excited to learn more about what you have to offer."

Ray glanced over at LaShonda and offered a subtle raise of his eyebrow. "Come on in and have a seat."

We made our way to Ray's office, and I couldn't help but notice something flicker in the man's eyes as he passed. I couldn't tell if he was concerned about LaShonda or perhaps even annoyed.

She seemed nervous about something, and he didn't like it.

We took a seat. I exchanged a look with Amos, who shrugged. I knew he sensed the tension that seemed to emanate in the office. Something was up.

Ray closed the door behind him and quickly moved behind his desk. I was sure LaShonda had told him about my questions. He may have been suspicious of our appointment, but we really did want to know about annuities.

Amos began asking questions about the different types of annuities available. I listened attentively, but my mind was already planning the questions I needed to ask.

When there was a lull in the conversation, I seized my opportunity. "Ray, I've been meaning to ask. How did you and LaShonda become partners in this business? I know you had a long career in the Army."

Ray leaned back in his chair, a smile played at the corners of his mouth. "Ah, well, LaShonda and I go way back. When I retired from the Army, I knew I wanted to do something different. It's such a different life going back to being a civilian."

Amos commented. "I know about that. Law enforcement seemed like a good fit for me. Did you think about it?"

Ray grinned. "Funny you ask. I did think about law enforcement, but I didn't want to have to wear a uniform every day. Plus, I'd had enough of putting my life on the line."

Amos laughed. "I hear that. You did enough to serve your country."

"Right, right. Anyhow, LaShonda and I reconnected. She told me how she got started with her business. I was pretty intrigued and I admired what she'd built, so I took some classes. She gave me a chance and then offered me a partnership. It seemed like the perfect fit."

I nodded, but something about his answer felt rehearsed, almost too perfect. "And how did Darren feel about you and LaShonda working together?"

At the mention of Darren's name, Ray's demeanor changed. His eyes hardened, and I could see the muscles in his jaw clench. "Darren," he spat, "was a fool. He never appreciated what he had with LaShonda. She's been so much better without him in her life."

The venom in his voice took me by surprise, and I could see Amos shifting uncomfortably in his seat. "I see," I said carefully. "It sounds like there was no love lost between you two."

Ray clenched his jaw as if stopping himself from saying what he really wanted to say. He smiled to regain his composure, but it seemed forced. "Darren and I had our differences, but that's all in the past now. So, how can we move forward with this service you're seeking?"

Even though Ray had changed the subject, the tension in the room remained palpable. There was definitely a fierce anger in this man toward Darren. But would he react violently if he had a reason to do that?

LaShonda divorced Darren and had clearly moved on with Ray.

I wanted to leave. I had an uncomfortable feeling that I couldn't put my finger on.

Almost like I sensed something was about to happen.

That's when raised voices floated through Ray's closed office door.

Chapter 26

Amos and I turned around at the sudden commotion outside Ray's office door. Raised voices filled the air. It sounded like one voice was LaShonda's and the other person was...

Ace.

Yes, that was her son's angry voice carrying through the thin walls.

"What did you do, Mom?"

"I can't believe this." Ray stood from the desk, making his black leather chair spin and hit the wall behind him. "Folks, I'm so sorry about this. Sit tight for a minute." Ray flung the door open and stepped out.

There was no way we were sitting in here. Amos sprang up first, with me behind him. We stood in the doorway to see the fireworks.

Jackie, the receptionist, sat riveted behind her desk, looking from her boss to her son.

Ace demanded. "What secret, Mom? What did Dad blackmail you about?"

LaShonda choked back her response, tears sliding down her face. "Ace, please, not here. Let's talk about this at home."

"No, Mom. You said, 'come to me and let's talk.' So, I'm here. Talk. I want to know the truth!" Ace shouted. "Dad came here to see you the night he died. What did you talk about?"

There was a moment of silence.

LaShonda flapped her mouth open and closed like a fish in water. "What are you talking about? I wasn't here that night, Ace. I was at a toastmaster's event. You know that... I've been talking about being the guest speaker for months."

Ace stared at his mother, his chest heaving. "His phone's location showed he came here. He even parked that stupid food truck around the corner from you."

"I gave your father money a few days before he died. He had no reason to come back here. I gave him what he asked for. We were good." LaShonda's voice trailed off. She spun around and focused on Ray. "I left early that day. Jackie left earlier than I did for a doctor's appointment." LaShonda visibly swallowed and then let out something like a sob. "Ray, you were the one who closed up that night. Did you see Darren?"

All of us turned to Ray.

He stood rigid, almost as if he'd lifted himself to his full height. The hardened look on his face confirmed everything I needed to know.

I reached for Amos's hand, not sure what the man was going to do.

But we should have been paying attention to the younger man.

Ace grabbed something off Jackie's desk. Before we could react, the young man slung the object at Ray. For someone they said wasn't coordinated enough to play sports, he knocked Ray off balance and the man landed on the floor.

"You killed my dad." With a ferocity that took my breath away, Ace pounced on the man and hit him.

Not willing to stay down, Ray shoved the young man off of him, sending him flying backwards.

LaShonda screamed.

I might have to.

Ray had a gash across his forehead where Ace had hit with what appeared to be a paperweight. Not deterred, the much larger man grabbed Ace. Next thing I knew, the man had Ace in a headlock.

I turned to Amos, who had his phone to his ear.

Was he calling 911? We needed to stop this before someone got hurt.

LaShonda ran over and started beating Ray on the back. "Let my son go. Let him go, right now."

The door to the office burst open. I don't know how Amos managed it, but the calvary had arrived.

In came Detective Wilkes, Chris and two deputies.

It took Chris and the two deputies a few minutes to manhandle Ray to the ground and cuff him. As the deputies dragged Ray outside, I heard him murmur the same thing over and over.

"He didn't deserve you. He didn't deserve you."

LaShonda had her arms around her son. Her tearstained face looked horrified as she watched Ray being led out. She started shaking her head. "I didn't know."

I walked over to her. "You should get an ambulance for Ace."

Ace lifted his head and pulled away from his mother. "I'm fine." He said, but his voice sounded weak from where Ray had him in a chokehold. "I need some air." He walked away from his mother and attempted to go outside. But Wilkes stopped him.

"Please stay," she said. "We need to talk to you, and I agree with Ms. Eugeena. You should get checked out. An ambulance will be here soon."

The office seemed to be overrun with many people suddenly. Amos went over to Chris and they conversed together about something. When Amos returned, he led me outside. "I told Chris that we would be across the street in the café if they needed anything from us. I don't know about you, but I could use a slice of sweet potato pie and a coffee."

That sounded like music to my ears. Food had always been a welcome diversion and comfort.

Inside the café, I sat while Amos placed our order. We didn't talk for a few moments, watching the activity across the street.

I finally had to ask. "Did you know Wilkes and Chris would show up?"

He nodded. "I told Chris about our plan to see Ray as soon as you made the appointment," he explained. "It turns out the ballistics report came back, and the same gun that killed Luke also killed Darren."

I felt a chill run down my spine. "Do you think Ray did it? Will they be able to connect the gun back to him? Why would he keep the weapon all this time?"

Amos shrugged. "I don't know all the details, but folks don't always get rid of murder weapons. For whatever reason, either they think they will never get caught or the weapon may have some meaning to them. I think they will find that Ray likes his firearms."

I thought back to the confrontation in the office, remembering the look of anger and betrayal on Ace's face. "I hope Ace and his mother can heal their relationship. I imagine LaShonda has a lot of regrets now. We still don't know what Darren blackmailed her about. Maybe we will never know."

"We have had quite a day." Amos said.

"I guess we can save the annuities discussion for another day."

Amos chuckled. "We will try again with another insurance agent."

"Mmm, one without murder in their back pocket."

It wasn't until the next day, Saturday, when Chris and Leesa came over that we found out the extent of what happened.

"Ray confessed," Chris said. "It was all him. He killed Luke by mistake, thinking he was Darren. Apparently, Darren had been refusing to sign the divorce papers and was giving LaShonda a hard time. He felt like LaShonda had cheated on him with Ray and kept trying to make things difficult. Back then, witnesses, one being Ace, saw the two men fighting days before Luke's death. In fact, Luke was the one to help break up the fight between Darren and Ray."

"Wow, so there was deep-rooted animosity between them."

Chris nodded. "But because of the neighborhood where Luke was shot, no one would have thought that he died from a case of mistaken identity."

Amos shook his head. "So Ray killed an innocent man and got away with it?"

Leesa had been sitting quietly. "He took away a son and a brother. The least he could have done was come forward. He had Marcus and his family in limbo, thinking they would never find out what happened to Luke."

"What I don't get was why try again? Of course, this time, he got his man. But why?"

Chris leaned forward. "You kind of nailed it, Ms. Eugeena. Darren started blackmailing LaShonda. Ray couldn't stand that. As long as Darren left LaShonda alone, it would have been fine."

"But what did LaShonda do?" Both Leesa and I asked at the same time.

We all laughed at our outbursts. Like mother, like daughter.

Chris finally said. "LaShonda isn't off the hook. The FBI is looking into LaShonda's business. There actually have been some complaints about insurance fraud from two of her clients. We won't know all the details for a while, but Darren was always into these get-rich-quick schemes that lost money. I think when she needed to start the business, LaShonda took some extreme measures. My guess is Darren knew about it and probably helped her."

"That's a shame. LaShonda spent all those years building that business on a rocky foundation."

Seemed like her mother and aunts were right, LaShonda certainly knew how to pick them.

"Alright, you two." I looked over at Leesa and Chris. "Now that Operation Food Truck Mystery has been solved, we have some wedding plans to finalize."

Amos and Chris exchanged glances and started laughing.

Leesa started giggling, too.

"What?" I asked.

Amos wiped his eyes. "I knew you were serious about solving mysteries, but when did you come up with case names?"

I shrugged. "You all are laughing, but I guessed this one."

Of course, I'm sure I had some help.

Thank you, Lord!

Chapter 27

Two months later

My heart swelled with pride and joy as I took in all the flowers surrounding the altar of Missionary Baptist Church. I sat beside Amos with rows of family and friends behind us. Junior had offered to help roll in Aunt Esther's wheelchair, but she decided to make use of her new walking cane. She walked slowly down the aisle with my Aunt Cora behind her. Both my aunts sat on the other side of Amos.

Junior and his wife Judy, along with their children, filled in the row behind us. The twin boys were as tall as their dad now. Seemed like every time I saw my oldest grandchildren, they'd grown another inch.

I exchanged looks with Chris's mom Belinda on the other side. She smiled back at me; her face looking happier than I'd seen in some time. She wasn't a woman who expressed emotion easily on her face. This was her only son's wedding, and I knew she was proud. I was too! My baby girl, Leesa, was about to walk down the aisle and start a new chapter in her life.

Looking to see who else joined us, I was delighted to see Detective Wilkes sitting on Chris's side of the aisle. At first, I was surprised. I didn't think I'd ever seen the detective in a dress before. But here she was in a pale yellow dress with her long red hair flowing around her shoulders instead of in the severe bun or ponytail that she usually wore. I smiled, glad to see her supporting Chris.

Once things had settled down from Operation Food Truck Mystery, we were all able to concentrate on the wedding, and Sasha and Marcus were getting a lot more business. They'd fed us ribs, corn on the cob, and loaded mashed potatoes last night for the rehearsal dinner. And I couldn't wait to taste the brisket that Marcus had prepared for the reception.

Despite what happened in the past month, Ace floated around the sanctuary, snapping photos. Leesa and Marcus were pleased with the bride and groom photos he'd taken of them out near the Charleston battery. The young man had so much talent and it was good to see him concentrating on himself. No one knew what his relationship was with Jada still, or even if there really was a question of paternity regarding Jada's son. But it was good to see the young man be mature about helping to support Jada and Dougie. Last I looked at the funding site, a good portion of money had been raised toward Dougie's medical care.

I wasn't sure if Annie Mae and Willie Mae would come. News of the FBI investigation of their niece's business had been circulating around the community. I glimpsed them midway back. After all, they had watched Leesa and my other children grow up at Missionary Baptist. If anything, we were a church family.

I looked further back and caught sight of Marcus and Sasha seated together in the congregation. A wave of relief washed over me knowing the dark cloud of suspicion that had once hung over them was a distant memory. I prayed each day for their family to continue to heal now that they knew the truth of Luke's death.

The piano player began playing. I would figure out who else attended later. It was time to focus on this day we'd all been waiting for.

Chris walked out from the side accompanied by his best man, CPD's newest detective, Andre Baez. I knew via the matchmaking efforts of Leesa and Chris, that the young man had been dating Joss for several months now. It was nice to see young people taking on connecting people together. That was something I enjoyed.

I turned to catch the processional. Kisha came down the aisle with her shy smile. I was so proud of her. I knew she wasn't used to having so many eyes on her, but she focused on leaving a trail of rose petals every few steps. Her white dress flowed out around her ankles, giving her the princess look she'd wanted. I'd noticed she was growing taller, coming a little above my hip now. Her baby cheeks were filling out into the girl she would soon blossom into.

Children grew up so fast.

Tyric practically ran down the aisle in his ring bearer suit, drawing chuckles and giggles along the way. He stopped in front of Chris, who reached out and rubbed his son's head.

Next were the bridesmaids, which included Carmen and Joss. I loved the pretty lavender dresses for the women and lavender cummerbunds and ties for the groomsmen that Leesa settled on.

As the music swelled, all eyes turned to the back of the church. There, standing tall and proud, was Leesa, her arm linked with her favorite brother, Cedric. My breath caught in my throat as I took in the sight of my beautiful daughter in her stunning white gown. She wasn't sure about wearing a sleeveless dress. She was self-conscience about her arms, but I reminded her it was her day. The dress was an excellent choice and looked very elegant on her.

Cedric, looking so much like his late father, beamed with pride as he escorted his little sister down the aisle.

Tears sprang to my eyes, and I dabbed at them. I knew Ralph was looking down on his baby girl.

Leesa reached the altar, her eyes locked with Chris's. The love between them was palpable as they exchanged vows and rings. Pastor Jones's voice rang out, clear and strong, "I now pronounce you husband and wife. You may kiss the bride!"

As Chris and Leesa sealed their union with a kiss, the congregation erupted in applause. "I present to you Mr. and Mrs. Christopher Black!" Pastor Jones announced, and the newlyweds turned to face their friends and family.

I leaned into Amos and whispered. "I want things to be normal from now on. No more mysteries for me."

He chuckled softly, his arm rubbing my shoulders. "I know. But we both know that if something catches your attention, you won't be able to resist investigating."

I smiled, knowing he was right. But for now, I would bask in the contentment that had settled over me. My children were all married now, each to a person who truly loved and cherished them. That's all a mother could want for her children.

About the Author

Tyora Moody is the author of **Soul-Searching Mysteries,** which includes **cozy mystery, women sleuth mystery, and mystery romance** under the Christian Fiction genre. Her books include the Eugeena Patterson Mysteries, Joss Miller Mysteries, Serena Manchester Mysteries, Reed Family Mysteries, and the Victory Gospel Mysteries.

When Tyora isn't working for a literary client, she's either loving on her cats, listening to an audiobook or podcast, binge-watching crime shows or Marvel movies, and of course, thinking about the next book.

To contact Tyora about reviewing her books or book club discussions, visit her online at TyoraMoody.com.

Join her newsletter at https://tyoramoody.substack.com/

Tyora Moody's Books

Eugeena Patterson Mysteries

Deep Fried Trouble, #1

Oven Baked Secrets, #2

Lemon Filled Disaster, #3

A Simmering Dilemma, #4

An Unsavory Mess, #5

A Spicy Predicament, #6

Marinated Conditions, #7

Eugeena Patterson Family Shorts

Shattered Dreams, #1

A Blended Family Christmas, #2

Falling in Love... Again!, #3

Joss Miller Mysteries

Double Mocha Blues, #1

A Latte Mayhem, #2

Serena Manchester Mysteries

Hostile Eyewitness, prequel

Bittersweet Motives, #1

Dangerous Confessions, #2

Waning Innocence, #3

Presumed Guilty, #4

Reed Family Mysteries

Broken Heart, #1

Troubled Heart, #2

Relentless Heart, #3

With All My Heart, #3.5

Faithful Heart, #4

Wounded Heart, #5

Victory Gospel Series (Mysteries)

When Rain Falls, #1

When Memories Fade, #2

When Perfection Fails, #3

MARINATED CONDITIONS

Victory Gospel Shorts (Sweet Romance)
The Replacement Date, #1
Southern Delights, #2
When Love Finds Me, #3
Nobody's Replacement, #4
A Southern Delights Christmas, #5
Holding on to Love, #6